Nidor.
*Nidor, one of two continents on a water-covered
planet.*
Nidor, a planet, a people, a nation.
Nidor, a religion . . .

THE SHROUDED PLANET

THE SHROUDED PLANET

ROBERT RANDALL

SF
ACE BOOKS, NEW YORK

An ACE Book

ISBN: 0-441-76219-0

First Ace printing: September 1982
Published simultaneously in Canada

Manufactured in the United States of America

2 4 6 8 0 9 7 5 3 1

Nidor.

Nidor, one of two continents on a water-covered planet.

Nidor, a planet, a people, a nation.

Nidor, a religion.

The primary was a B class star, a huge, blue-white stellar engine, pouring out its radiation at a rate that made Earth's yellow Sol look picayune by comparison. The planet Nidor swung round its sun at a distance so great that it took nearly three thousand years for the world to complete one revolution—and even so, the planet was hot. The continents, on the Eastern hemisphere just south of the equator, had a mean temperature of 110° Fahrenheit, and continually sweltered beneath the eternal cloud layer that swathed the planet.

Of solid land there was little; more than eighty-five percent of the planet's surface was covered by the shallow sea.

It had not always been so. Geological evidence indicated that the planet had recently gone through a period of upheaval, during which whole continents had sunk beneath the waters.

It had happened within historical time, some four or five thousand years previous to the planet's discovery by Earth. It was upon the legend of the happenings at the time of the Cataclysm that the religion of the surviving Nidorians was based. Before the Cataclysm, the planet had evolved humanoids very similar physically to man: to the eye the only major difference was that instead of the irregular distribution of hair over the human body, the Nidorian was fairly evenly covered with light, curly down that ranged in color from platinum blonde to light brown.

When the Cataclysm occurred, the sole remaining group of civilized beings on the planet were on the continent of Nidor—and they had carried with them a myth of the terror of the Great Cataclysm, and of demons that lived beyond the sea.

And thus they were when they were discovered by the roving interstellar scout ships of Man—*Earthman.*

240th CYCLE

I

The Cyclic Day of the Great Cataclysm had arrived once again. Sixteen periods of sixteen days constituted a Nidorian year. And sixteen years made a full cycle, when each of the sixteen Clans of Nidor had been named.

And traditionally, each cycle began with the first day of the first period of the Year of Yorgen—according to the Scripture, the Day of the Great Cataclysm.

Grandfather Kinis peCharnok Yorgen, Elder Leader, Priest-Mayor of the Holy City of Gelusar, Supreme Councillor of the Elders—and therefore the highest secular authority on Nidor—stood before the high altar of the Great Temple of the Great Light, raised his golden-haired arms, crossed them at the wrists in benediction, and intoned:

"And thus, on the day of the Great Cataclysm, we both rejoice and mourn. We mourn that the Great Light felt it necessary to kill so many of His people, but we rejoice that the unrighteous were taken from Nidor and the righteous remained, to be led to Holy Gelusar by the Lawyer Bel-rogas Yorgen.

"And because of the Holy Righteousness of our Ancestors, I, a Priest of the Great Light, give you, on this solemn day, a most solemn blessing."

He had timed it perfectly. At exactly that moment, the beams of the Great Light, bursting through the thick cloud layer and collected and focused by the huge lens in the roof of the Temple, struck the central pit of the high altar and the aromatic herbs began to smoke. Within a few seconds, as the heat's intensity increased, the herbs burst into flame. When the flames died, after a short space of time, the Celebration of the Great Cataclysm was over for another sixteen years, and the two hundred and fortieth Year of Yorgen had begun.

While the great crowd of participants in the Temple—and the even greater crowd gathered in the Square of Holy Light outside the Temple—murmured their final prayers, Grandfather Kinis peCharnok, Elder of the Clan of Yorgen, strode away from the high altar, his arms folded in reverence.

He walked down the aisle, his head held high, as the people chanted their prayers, repeating them, as tradition demanded, sixteen times. As each Clan was remembered, the Elder Grandfather raised his arms and crossed his wrists in benediction, and as the final Clan, Tipell, was mentioned, he found himself at the door of the Great Temple, facing outward toward the people gathered in the Square of Holy Light.

Again he raised his arms. "May we obey the Scripture and the Law, and may we follow in the Way of our Ancestors," he said sonorously.

"In the Way of our Ancestors," the crowd repeated.

And then something happened which had never before been seen on Nidor—a planet which doted on tradition, and shunned unprecedented events. The figure of the Elder Leader suddenly was wrapped in a nimbus of blue-white light, and, his hands still raised in benediction, he floated into the air and rapidly vanished into the cloud-laden sky.

The worshippers, stricken dumb with religious awe, could do nothing but stare at their disappearing Elder Leader.

Grandfather Kinis peCharnok was badly frightened. He didn't know what was happening to him. Suddenly, without warning, his limbs had become frozen, his body weightless.

Like a leaf from a peych-bean plant lifted by the morning wind, he found himself drifting upwards toward the cloud layer that glowed above him—upwards toward the Great Light.

It was too much for him; even though he was unable to move a muscle of his body, he still was not an absolute prisoner. He could still react, in the one way he had left open to him. He did so.

He fainted.

Later, words drifted through his mind.

"Kinis peCharnok, open your eyes!"

Grandfather Kinis heard the words, but at first they made no sense. All he could feel was the sheer terror of weightlessness and the awful horror of unsupported floating.

Then he realized that he was *not* floating. His back was solidly supported by a soft padding, not unlike the bed in the Temple to which he was used.

He took a deep breath. Still, he kept his eyes firmly closed.

Demons? Who knows?

"Kinis peCharnok," said a soft, gentle, definitely strange voice, "We are your friends. There's no reason to be afraid of us."

Kinis peCharnok gingerly opened his eyes—just the barest slit. And then he closed them again, frightened, unsure of what he had seen.

What were they? Were they men? No. Not, at least, good, honest, Nidorian men. Their faces were bare—pink and shiny—except for the curious tufts of hair on their chins and the tops of their heads.

"Kinis peCharnok, we are your friends," the voice repeated.

The old priest opened his eyes in time to see who was speaking.

"Who—who are you?" he asked, trying to keep his voice steady.

"My name is McKay," the weird being said, speaking with barely a trace of accent. "I am an Earthman."

"Earthman? A man of the soil?"

The strange one chuckled softly. "I guess that's about as close as we can come."

Kinis peCharnok was an old man; he had served his people as Elder Leader for more than two cycles. He was learned, for in nearly forty years—two cycles and a half—he had learned nearly all that was necessary for an Elder of the Council to learn. And yet, the self styled "Earthman" simply did not speak sense; he was as foolish and undecipherable in his speech as the two-year-old child of a deestkeeper.

"As close as you can come?" Kinis repeated uncomprehendingly.

"There's no better way of saying it with the words you know," explained the thing that had called itself McKay. "In our own language, it's—" And he spoke two short syllables.

"*Your* language? You have your own? There is but one language! But—" Suddenly the priest grew angry. "Why have you taken me away from my people and my Temple?" he asked with dignity.

"You were chosen," said McKay.

"Chosen? For what?" He sat up on the pallet and looked wildly around. "Where have you taken me? Where am I?" He paused, then in a soft voice uttered the question that had been concerning him since he had awakened. "Am I dead?"

Another of the Earthmen smiled. "Not dead, Aged and Most Ancient Grandfather."

"No," said McKay. "We have brought you here so that we could speak in privacy and without disturbance."

"But I came up! I floated up! I must be near the Great Light Himself!"

"Not greatly nearer," the Earthman said without smiling. "You're in a ship, floating in the cloud layer. The Great Light is far above that."

Incredulously Kinis said, "You have seen the Great Light—face to face?"

"We have seen Him. But the more closely one approaches Him, the more unbearable is His light for human eyes."

Kinis peCharnok sat quietly, head bowed, thinking. They had told him he was in a ship. That was simple enough to grasp: ships sailed the rivers, brought produce from Gelusar southward to Tammulcor, travelled between the mainland and the Bronze Islands—yes, he knew what a ship was. But a ship in the clouds—and such a ship!

The walls were of metal—yes, of metal, shining, silvery, so bright the priest could see the reflection of his own weary, silver-downed face in them. Gleaming colored lights dotted the ceiling; arching spans of metal bridged the air. It was a strange-looking ship, indeed.

And its crew had seen the Great Light.

Kinis peCharnok felt absolute certainty that they spoke the truth. The things these people did were magical—a ship that flew the sky!—and the Great Light was the source of all magic. The magic of the growing peych-bean, the magic of the nightly rains that ground down the mountain-tops, the magic of a woman bearing children—all these were the magic of the Great Light.

And these beings had seen Him!

Kinis peCharnok began to tremble, realizing he had been chosen for something strange and wonderful.

He said, "What do you want with me?"

"Your help in doing the Will of the Great Light," said McKay. "We have been sent by Him to bring your people closer to Him. In order to bring your people to the Light, it has been decided that a school shall be built near Holy Gelusar."

The priest frowned. "There already is a school in Gelusar. Does a city need two schools?"

"Not *in* Gelusar," McKay said. "Our school must be outside the city proper— close enough to the Great Temple, but far from city congestion. It must be surrounded by peaceful groves where the students can relax. Besides, this will be a special school. Aside from teaching the Law and the study of Scripture, we intend to give courses in natural sciences, engineering, and agriculture."

"But why do you need me?"

"Many problems face us. The land must be procured. The school buildings must be built. Before that, our presence must be announced. The people must be prepared for our coming, and for the school. And that will be your job, Ancient Grandfather.'' McKay looked squarely at him. ''You will do this for us—and for the Great Light.''

II

In the High Council room within the Great Temple at Gelusar, the Elder Vyless, Councillor of the Clan Vyless and second only to Elder Leader Kinis peCharnok in point of venerable age, placed the tips of the fingers of his right hand against those of his left.

He looked unseeingly at the tent they formed when he held them on his chest. "But, Most Aged One," he said without looking up, "If what you say is true—"

"*If?*" The tone of the Elder Leader's voice was sharp. "You have heard others testify that they saw me lifted into the air. You have heard me tell what these Earthmen wish to do for us. Do you imply that I lie?"

The Elder Vyless lifted a hand. "Oh, no, Ancient One. I would never imply any such thing. But—and I offer no offense here—is it possible that you are mistaken, perhaps?"

Elder Grandfather Kinis peCharnok narrowed his eyes. He saw Vyless' motivation, and he did not like it.

The Elder Vyless had been waiting years for the death of Elder Leader Kinis peCharnok Yorgen, so he

11

could succeed to the Leadership. Of late, he had become increasingly irritable as his own health had shown signs of waning, while the Elder Leader seemed more youthful than ever. It became increasingly clear that if matters went on as they had, the Elder Vyless would not live to see the death of his superior. And this knowledge, Kinis peCharnok thought, made the Elder Vyless more and more bitter.

Kinis peCharnok knew Vyless' position, and could appreciate his feelings. But he could only put up with so much of the Elder's sly needling before he became somewhat sharp with him.

He swivelled to face the Elder Vyless. "And how, just how might I be mistaken?" he asked. "Did I dream it all, then? And did everyone else dream it?"

Instantly the Elder Vyless bent his hand in a ritual gesture of apology. "I didn't mean that, Elder Leader. I believe you saw what you say you saw."

"Well, then?"

"Have you ever considered the possibility that these beings might be lying to you?"

Kinis peCharnok's eyes widened. "Agents of the Great Light *lying*, you say? That comes dangerously close to blasphemy—youth!"

Youth! The Elder Vyless flushed at the insult, but he dared not argue with his superior. Taking a deep breath, he said, "Ancient and Venerable One, if a group of demons from the Outer Darkness were to come here, would they not tell us that they came from the Great Light?"

Kinis peCharnok rose and glared down the brightly-polished table at the gaunt, hard features of the Elder Vyless. Choosing his words with some restraint, the Elder Leader said, "You're evidently not thinking well this day, Elder Vyless. Consider: how, may I ask, could a demon of the Darkness lift up a praying priest in the middle of the day—indeed, right after Midmeal Services? I'm afraid your doctrinal theology is weak, Elder. Your argument lacks backbone. Demons can tempt the righteous in the daytime, but they certainly cannot manifest themselves.''

The Elder Yorgen paused, watching Vyless stiffen. In the space of minutes, his Elder Leader had called him both youthful and unlearned, before several other members of the Council. But, as Kinis peCharnok waited, his authority asserted itself: Vyless' anger faded, as he realized that it was wrong to question the judgment of the Elder Leader.

There was a sharp rap at the door, breaking the tension. At the Elder Leader's command, the door opened and a yellow-clad acolyte stepped in.

"Well?" Kinis peCharnok asked impatiently.

"Ancient Leader, the Aged Elder Grandfather Dran peBor Gormek would see you.''

"I'm speaking with the Elder Vyless now. Tell the Elder Gormek to wait for me in my office; I'll be with him as soon as I'm free.''

He turned back to the Elder Vyless. Speaking quietly he said, "I would appreciate your aid in the matter of the land. Come here.''

He led the way to the window.

Below them spread the Holy City of Gelusar, the City of the Great Light Himself. It clustered around a bend in the broad Tammul River, which could be seen shining in the distance, spanned by bridges.

"The school must not be in the city,'' Kinis peCharnok said. "The Earthmen said it must be near the city, but separated from it. You will buy, therefore, a proper tract of land from the estates across the river. It must be good land, suitable for growing trees and hedges, for the Earthmen specifically said that they wished the school to be located in a pleasant park.''

"Why?" Vyless asked.

The Elder Yorgen shrugged. "So they said—and so it must be.''

"The Council has already approved this matter, and I won't question it," Vyless muttered. "But what else would you have me do?''

"Pay the usual Temple price for the land. I'll give you a note for a withdrawal from the cobalt reserves for it. There shouldn't be any problems.''

"Is that all?''

"Yes. Will you do this for me, Elder Vyless?''

Vyless was a beaten man. His now was the responsibility of locating the school. "It shall be as you say, Elder Leader.''

"Good. The Peace of your Ancestors be with you always.''

"And may the Great Light illumine your mind as He does the world, Elder Leader," came the automatic ritual response.

They departed together, Vyless heading for the main stairway. Kinis peCharnok turned off into his own small, austere office, where the Elder Gormek was waiting for him.

Elder Grandfather Dran peBor Gormek was a short, broad-chested man who hailed originally from the Bronze Islands, the small island group which lay west of the continent of Nidor, not far off the mainland. Dran peBor was cultured of speech, although occasionally, in moments of great stress and excitement, his voice was liable to betray him by slipping into the Bronze Island dialect he had spoken as a child.

"I ask your blessing, Elder Leader," he said, rising as Kinis peCharnok entered.

The Elder Leader offered a brief word and gesture. Then Dran peBor said, "I have come to ask you about the money you've assessed to the Clan Gormek, Ancient One. It seems a little stiff to me."

Kinis peCharnok smiled. "The assessment is for the school, Elder Gormek."

"Exactly," the Elder Gormek said. "My Clan might be—ah—somewhat reluctant to contribute good weights for the building of yet another school."

Kinis peCharnok had foreseen the situation, and he was prepared for it. The Clan Gormek was unique in that its members were located in just one geographical area—they were nearly all Bronze Islanders, miners and sailors. Separated as they were from the Council-dominated life of the mainland, they were not as devoted in their religious duties as they might be.

"My Clan is poor—" the Elder Gormek continued, but Kinis peCharnok interrupted quickly.

"Not that poor, Elder Gormek. Let's not delude ourselves. They give little to the Temple, it's true, but it isn't poverty that causes it. It's lack of discipline, pure and simple."

The Elder Gormek inclined his head. "I admit the defect, Ancient One. Sailors especially pay only perfunctory homage to the Rites of the Great Light. Many of them don't see the inside of a temple more than once a year—and some—well, some less frequently."

"And as for the poverty your sailors plead—" the Elder Leader began.

"Sailors make good wages, too. But it's difficult to get them to part with it, Elder Grandfather. And I'm thinking specifically of the mining population of the

Islands. The digging of copper and zinc and tin from the ground is not as lucrative as it might be. Even the most religious of them can't afford to give much.'' The Elder Gormek paused, then added: ''And even the most religious will be somewhat reluctant to give extra for a school which they will never see.''

The Elder Leader shook his head. ''There's no reason why they shouldn't. The Earthmen specifically told me that anyone on Nidor who passes the school's entrance examinations can enter. *Anyone*.''

''Sailors, even? Miners?''

''If they take the exam. The Earthmen want students in excellent physical condition, and they tell me they plan to give the candidates a special test to discover their mental potentialities. If they are capable of learning, they will be taught whatever is necessary. Surely,'' Kinis peCharnok concluded slyly, ''the Clan Gormek has many such people.''

''It does,'' returned the Elder Gormek with a touch of pride.

''Very well, then. Explain it to them and they will pay. I'm using the cobalt reserves for ready cash, but you're aware of what would happen if this money weren't replaced. Our economic system would be unbalanced—and this must not happen. To replace the cash, we have to depend on the Temple Tax. And it is *your* job to see that the Clan Gormek pays their Temple Tax.''

Dran peBor shrugged. ''They'll pay, Elder Leader. I don't doubt that. But I feel the amount is a bit heavy, perhaps.''

''Apportion it out. Get more from the sailors if the miners have so little. *But get it*.''

''I will see to it, Ancient One,'' said the Elder Gormek, sighing almost imperceptibly.

"Excellent. May the Peace of your Ancestors be with you always."

"And may the Great Light illumine your mind as He does the world," responded the Elder Gormek. He nodded, turned, and left Kinis peCharnok's office.

The Elder Leader remained behind his desk, thinking. The obstacles were falling; the school would soon be built. It was good to think that in *his* time, during his stay in the Council's highest seat, this had happened. The Earthmen had come, to lead Nidor to the Great Light.

The necessary cash would be raised soon enough, Kinis peCharnok thought. True, it seemed to be increasingly difficult to get enough money to run the temples properly, these days. Each person gave the right amount, as they always had, but there weren't as many people on Nidor as there had been many cycles ago. For some reason, the birth rate seemed to be dropping off.

The Elder Leader shrugged. The Great Light guided them always. The Great Light had brought the Earthmen. His plan must be followed, and the Way of the Ancestors be observed.

III

Elder Vyless did his job well, if without enthusiasm. The necessary land was selected and purchased from the funds appropriated by the Council. The plans that the Earthmen had given to the Elder Leader were handed over to the stonemasons and the builders.

It was on the day of the Feast of the Sixteen Clans that the ground was formally dedicated. The people had been warned to expect great things on that day, and they came from miles to see the anticipated miracles.

Miracles. They had not been heard of since the legendary days right after the Cataclysm. There had been miracles then, as everyone knew, and as the Scriptures attested.

And now, it seemed, the Great Light once again was taking a visible means of showing His love for His people.

On the day of the dedication the land was crowded with men and women of all clans and all classes, come in from everywhere in the province of Dimay, some even from Sugon to the north, Thyvash and Pelvash to

the south, and a few from the westerly province of
Lebron.

The farmers rode great, heavily-muscled deests,
animals with broad shoulders fitted for pulling plows
rather than riding. The priests and the laughing, joking
merchants rode in on slim racing deests, their bony legs
flashing as they brought their three-toed hooves down
on the turf and lifted them again, prancing smartly, with
their arched necks held proudly high.

One area of the field had been closed off with stout
ropes of braided peych-fiber; within this area, no one
was permitted to go. Yellow-robed acolytes stood by to
ward off the curious.

The day wore on; the crowd gathered. Kinis peCharnok Yorgen had seen to it that Nidorians of all kinds,
from every stratum of life, would be present. The
miners of the Bronze Islands had sent a delegation;
farmers busy with their crops of peych had come up the
Tammul and eastward down the Vash.

At Midmeal, the Elder Leader stepped forward to
conduct the Midmeal Services. They were held on a
small portable altar that had been brought over from
Gelusar's secondary temple, the Kivar, and an acolyte
held a miniature burning glass, to remind the people of
the use of such a lens long ago by the Great Lawyer,
Bel-rogas Yorgen, who had led the people after the
Cataclysm so many thousands of years before.

The ceremony ended. Kinis peCharnok drew back
from the altar. The time had come, he knew, for the
Earthmen to appear, and his sense of timing was as
acute as it had always been. He looked upward.

The assemblage followed him. He raised his eyes to
the sky, narrowing them to shield them from the awful
glare of the Great Light as He shone through the ever-
present clouds of Nidor.

At first, nothing could be seen but the glare and the pearly-gray background of cloud. Then a gasp went up from the crowd, spreading rapidly as person after person saw the swiftly-expanding dot.

They had been told to expect a ship. But this was a ship such as none on Nidor had ever seen before.

They knew ships, ships made of wood, with masts and sails. But this was of metal, and it was surrounded by an ethereal blue nimbus. The ship was not large, as ships went. It was a tapering, rounded cylinder some forty feet in length, perhaps twelve feet thick. Slowly, like a soaring sea-lizard, it settled gently to the ground in the center of the roped-off area.

A door in its side opened.

An Earthman appeared.

Almost automatically, the entire crowd, man by man, bent in a reverent bow. There could be no doubt now that this was the magic of the Great Light.

After a long moment, during which the Earthman's searching eyes roved over the crowd, he spoke. He held something small and metallic near his lips, and his voice thundered over the crowd.

"My name is Jones," he said. "I am an Earthman. May the Great Light illumine your mind, that you may see the truth of His Word."

He paused, while the answering murmur rustled through the crowd. "And may you walk in the Way of your Ancestors."

After a moment he continued. "You come here today to see ground dedicated for a school. Some of you, probably, are wondering why we are here, and why we are building this school. And it is not to be thought odd that you wonder. I will explain, and I would have you think long on my words.

"There comes a time in the history of any people,"

Jones said, "when they find themselves becoming too self-satisfied. They believe that they are doing their best, but the Great Light demands more of them. They may know the Law and the Scriptures fairly well, but the Great Light demands that they study them even more closely.

"That time has arrived for Nidorians. In order to follow the Law as the Great Light meant it to be followed, the Law must be studied more closely. What does it *really* mean? What is the real meaning of the precepts which the Great Light would have us follow?

"The Scriptures, too, must be studied; they tell a story, a history. What is the Great Light trying to tell us in that story? What message is He trying to give us? Are we doing enough in our efforts to understand ourselves and Him?

"To really understand one's religion, it is necessary to correlate it with the facts of the world around one. And that will be the purpose of this school. The students that attend here will be taught the Law and the Scripture, and their uses in everyday life. They will be taught the facts of nature, things that men need to know and understand in order to reach a greater understanding of the True Nature of the Great Light.

"Thus, we will come to know Him better.

"And, in honor of the Lawgiver who knew Him so well, this school will be named for the Great Lawyer who brought the people of Nidor safely out of harm at the time of the Cataclysm. Henceforth, this land will be known as the Bel-rogas School of Divine Law, in eternal honor of the Lawyer, Bel-rogas Yorgen."

Jones paused for a moment, then he said, "When the task of building the school is finished, we will return and begin our teaching. We will select the wisest of the Priesthood to assist us, and those students who pass our rigid entrance examinations will inaugurate their studies with us.''

Turning, Jones re-entered the strange ship. Silently the door swung shut.

The ship lifted again—toward the Realm of the Great Light.

* * *

The Bel-rogas School of Divine Law was built rapidly, but with care.

Each building was constructed exactly according to the detailed specifications of the Earthmen. They were lovely buildings, high, vaulting, surrounded by the spacious parks Jones had spoken of.

And when the job of construction was done, Jones and his fellow Earthmen returned as they had promised. This time they came, not in their ship, but floating down by themselves, each surrounded by a pale blue aura which winked out as soon as their feet touched the ground. It made an impressive spectacle.

Those were Light-touched days on Nidor. With representatives of the Great Light actually on the planet, working with the Council, travelling through the land from Thyvash to Lebron, it was as if the Light shone a little brighter on Nidor.

From the very beginning, the School was successful. From the day the first class, five hundred strong, men and women, the pride of Nidor, entered the gate that led to the School grounds, the School was hailed by all.

Great, colorful ceremonies were held on feast days. The students soon became widely known for their piety and learning. When they returned to their homes during the annual recess, they were regarded with awe and respect by their families; youngsters, seeing the re-

turned scholars, were fired with the ambition of studying at Bel-rogas themselves.

It was not easy to be accepted by the Bel-rogas
School of Divine Law. Only those young men and
women who were physically in excellent condition and
mentally active and wholesome were permitted to
enroll—and even then, if the candidate came from a
line known for sickness or inheritance of some disease,
he would be sorrowfully turned away. Standards were
high—but those who graduated were the finest of the
young people of Nidor.

Marriages among the students were common. And,
more often than not, the children born of such marriages expressed a desire to study at Bel-rogas almost as
soon as they were old enough to talk.

Time rolled by. As had been expected, the Elder
Leader, Grandfather Kinis peCharnok Yorgen, out-
lived the Elder Vyless by three years, and was succeeded by a priest of his own clan, the Elder Grandfather Yorgen peDom Yorgen. The Yorgens had always been known for their longevity, which was not
surprising, since they could trace their ancestry back to
the incredibly long-lived Bel-rogas Yorgen.

As the years passed, the stature of the School grew
even greater. Many of its graduates trained especially
for the priesthood, and became learned judges of the
court; it was expected that in the course of time they
would succeed to the Council. Others became successful merchants whose fairness in business dealings was
renowned.

And the School grew, and prospered, and Nidor was
happy that the Great Light had sent the Earthmen.

Kiv peGanz Brajjyd had no way of knowing that he

was marked for a special destiny, when he made his decision to enter the School.

His father was a farmer, moderately wealthy, a devout man and a good farmer. He held large acreage near Kandor, in the Province of Thyvash. Old Ganz was anxious for his oldest son to follow in his footsteps, and manage the farm which had made the family comfortable for so many generations.

But Kiv would have none of it. He insisted that the management of the farm should eventually be turned over to his younger brother, Kresh peGanz; Kiv, himself, had an eye on the priesthood.

"Very well," old Ganz said, sighing unhappily. He was a shrewd man, and saw that he would gain nothing by thwarting Kiv. "Enter the priesthood, if you can. But I insist that you study at the Bel-rogas School."

"I had planned to," Kiv said.

"Well enough. Should they refuse you—should you be unable to pass the entrance requirements, or if you fail to complete your training—then you're to return to Kandor and settle on the farm, as you should."

"And if I graduate, father?"

"Then you can go on into the priesthood—with my blessing."

Kiv had little doubt about his ability to enter the School. Physically and mentally, he was in excellent condition. He was confident that there would be no problems keeping him from the School.

The Earthmen agreed with him. He travelled up from Thyvash to Holy Gelusar and submitted himself to the entrance requirements; he was duly enrolled. Within the first year of his studies, he had met and proposed to one of the most beautiful—to his mind—of the girl students. She was Narla geFulda Sesom.

At the end of the first year, he took her home with him to Kandor to meet his parents. But he was impatient to return to the School. They cut short their vacation and set out once again for Gelusar, and the Belrogas School.

KIV

I

The hard, savage mandibles of the hugl slashed at
Kiv peGanz Brajjyd and missed. Kiv jerked his hand
out of the beast's way just in time. Again the hugl
lashed out—and this time, the animal connected. The
powerful jaws came together; Kiv's blood spurted
down over the creature's head.

"Damn," he snapped, irritated.

The animal's little teeth had taken a nasty bite out of
the ball of his thumb. Before the hugl could snap again,
Kiv dropped it into the little wooden box he usually
carried with him for just this purpose, and clicked the
lid shut.

"Bite you?" his wife Narla asked.

"Yes. Nasty little beast," Kiv said without rancor.
"I should have learned how to handle them by now. If
they're all as hungry as this one, I can see why they're
having so much trouble with them on the northern
farms."

He turned the box over. The bottom, which was
made of glass, permitted him to see the hugl. Clashing
its jaws, the inch-long creature scrambled madly
around the inside of the hard, plastic-impregnated box.

Narla iKiv geFulda Sesom, who had only recently
been privileged to add the ''iKiv'' that denoted marriage to her name, looked with interest at the little box
in her husband's hand.

''What's so different about it, Kiv?''

''The armor,'' he told her. ''It's black. I've never
seen a black one before. All the specimens I have in my
lab at the School are brown.'' He wrapped his pocket
kerchief around the nipped thumb and tied it. ''Take
this thing, will you?''

He handed the box up to her, and she stared at it
curiously. Kiv dug his high-heeled riding boot into the
stirrup and pulled himself up to the saddle. ''Jones will
be interested in that specimen,'' he said, as they guided
their deests out of the roadside thicket where they had
paused for midmeal. ''Put it in the saddlebag. And be
sure to remind me to show it to Jones, as soon as we're
back at the School.''

She nodded and reached back obediently to stow the
box in the leather pouch. Kiv felt a glow of pleasure as
he watched the smooth play of her muscles under the
fine golden down that covered her skin.

Since she was clad, as he was, in the traditional
Nidorian dress—sleeveless vest and thigh-length
shorts—he had no thought about the beauty of her
clothing; it was her own beauty he saw. She might not
be the most beautiful girl on Nidor, but she approached
Kiv's personal ideal well enough to satisfy him.

He tipped his head back and squinted at the eternally
clouded sky. The Great Light was almost at His

brightest, spreading His effulgence magnificently over the green countryside. It was a little after midday.

The Earthman, Jones, said that the Great Light was a "blue-white star." Just what a star was, Kiv didn't know. They were supposed to be above the cloud layer. Some of the things Jones said didn't make much sense, Kiv thought. But it was better than two cycles since they had arrived on Nidor and made themselves known to Grandfather Kinis peCharnok Yorgen, and the Earthmen had said many strange things in that time.

"We've got about an hour's ride ahead of us," Kiv remarked. "If we make good time, that is. I can't wait to see the School again, Narla. This vacation seemed to last forever."

"You've been terribly anxious to get back to work, haven't you? I felt it all the time you were home. You seemed so anxious to leave that I almost felt like apologizing to your parents. But—"

"The School is very important to me, Narla. I don't have to tell you that." It was a great honor to be chosen to study at the Earthmen's School, and Kiv was conscious of that.

"Of course, silly. I know," Narla said.

Kiv snapped the reins, and his deest broke into a smooth trot, its long legs pistoning up and down. Narla's mount kept pace easily.

"How long will it be before you write your book?" she asked. "I mean, do you think you'll manage to get the rest of the data you need this term? Seems to me you've covered the hugl about as thoroughly as the little creatures deserve to be covered."

Kiv nodded. "I think I'm nearly done. It's going to be a rather scholarly thing, I'm afraid; no one is very interested in the life cycle of the hugl. Otherwise someone at the School would have thought of the project long before I did.''

"I know. But your work is still good training for you, even if it's not terribly important," Narla said. "As the Scripture says, 'The observation of life permits one to attain an inner peace.' ''

Kiv frowned. "I'm not sure the Scripture means that. I don't think they were talking about lower forms of life.''

"Of course they were! It says 'life,' doesn't it? And if a hugl isn't alive, I don't know what it is.''

Kiv grinned and rode on silently for a while, resting lightly in the saddle while his deest carried him at a swift pace over the matted turf of the road.

Finally he said, ''It may be so. Certainly Jones was all in favor of my studying the hugl as my big project. And I don't think Jones would permit anything that violated the Word of the Scriptures. Hoy! What's that?''

Narla, startled by his sudden change of tone, glanced quickly at him. Kiv was pointing down the road with one golden arm outstretched.

Someone stood in the middle of the road, just where it forked. As they drew nearer, they saw it was a man, in the familiar blue tunic of a priest, who held up his hand as Kiv and his wife approached. The two riders pulled their animals to a halt and bowed their heads reverently.

"The peace of your Ancestors be with you always,'' said the priest ritually.

"And may the Great Light illumine your mind as He does the world, Grandfather,'' Kiv and Narla chanted together.

"How may we serve you, Grandfather?'' asked Kiv.

"By carrying a message. Did you intend to cross the Bridge of Klid?"

Kiv nodded. He took careful notice of the other man. The priest was not too much older than Kiv himself, and was evidently a recent graduate of one of the priestly Schools—perhaps even Bel-rogas. His bearing had all the dignity that was proper to his office.

"Yes, we were going to use the bridge," Kiv said.

The Grandfather shook his head. "I'm afraid you'll have to use the Bridge of Gon and go through the city, my son. The Bridge of Klid is being repaired."

Kiv barely managed to conceal a frown. Another delay! And, of course, the proper thing for him to do would be to offer his services in the repair work. He began to think he would never get back to the School.

"If you would do so," the priest went on, "it would be appreciated if you could go to the nearest communicator and tell the City Fathers that we need more men to help repair the bridge. Give them my name: Dom peBril Sesom."

"I'll be glad to. What happened, Grandfather?"

"A section of the roadbed near the center has collapsed. We want to get the job done before the evening traffic begins."

"I see," Kiv said. "Very well, Grandfather. My wife and I will go on to the city and get hold of a communicator. Then I'll come back and help with the work. My wife can go on to the School."

The priest's reaction was an immediate one. "The School? The Bel-rogas School?"

Kiv nodded.

Frowning, the priest said, "In that case I don't see how I can take up your time with bridge repair work. Your studies are much more important. *Anyone* can

repair a bridge; only a few can assimilate the Scriptures
and the Law. And,'' he added, a faint wistfulness in his
voice that told Kiv much, ''Even fewer are worthy of
studying at Bel-rogas. Go and give my message to the
City Fathers, and then continue on to the School.''

''Very well, Grandfather.''

The priest raised one hand in benediction. ''Go, with
the blessings of the Great Light, and Those Who have
passed on to His Realm.''

Leaving the priest, Kiv and Narla turned their deests
and took the southern branch of the road toward the
great city of Gelusar, a long ribbon of a road curling
through the gray-green farmlands.

''Nuisance,'' Narla said.

''What is?''

''This business of treating us as if we were likely to
melt in the first rainfall. Did you see the way he looked
at you when you said we were from the School? 'Your
studies are of greater importance,' she mimicked. 'I can
not permit you to work on the bridge.' And I'll wager
that's what you wanted him to say, too. You didn't
want to work on that bridge, but you had to offer for the
sake of courtesy. You just want to get back to the
School, and Jones.''

''*Narla!*''

He speared her with an angry scowl. ''When a
Grandfather tells you something—'' he began.

''I know,'' she said, crestfallen. ''I'm sorry.''

They rode on in silence for a while, Kiv brooding
over Narla's lapse of taste. Kiv prided himself on his
keen sense of the right; he believed that was why he had
been chosen for the School, and he hoped that someday
it would place him on the Council of Elders.

The road to the Bridge of Gon was a narrow, winding

one, and Kiv's deest required considerable guiding at each turn. A stupid animal, Kiv reflected, as for what seemed the twentieth time in the last ten minutes he put pressure on the reins to turn the deest.

"Narla?" he said after a while. "Narla, that's the second time I've heard you question a Grandfather's instructions since we left my parents. And I don't like it—not at all."

"I'm sorry, I told you. Why can't you leave it at that?"

"But the tone of your voice when you mimicked him!" Kiv protested. "Narla, don't you know what respect means?"

"All I wanted to know is why we're so sacred," she said petulantly. "As soon as he found out we were from Bel-rogas, we suddenly became too important to help repair the bridge. *Why?*"

"Because we've been chosen, Narla. Only a few are chosen. And the Law, Narla—that's what's important. The Grandfather told you: anyone can fix a bridge. We're special."

The Earthmen had come from the sky—from the stars, Jones said, whatever *they* were—from the Great Light Himself, for all Kiv knew. The Earthmen were there to teach; his job was to learn.

"I'm sorry," Narla said a third time. "I'm only a woman, I guess. I don't understand these things."

Be patient, Kiv thought wearily. *Patient.*

After a long spell of hard riding, they eased up on their tired deests to rest them for the final lap of the journey.

Narla had said nothing all this time. Finally she asked: "Is Jones *really* from the sky? I mean, is it true that the Earthmen come from the Great Light?"

She keeps asking questions like a small child who's too impatient to sit still, Kiv thought. *It's been a long trip; she's tired.*

"I don't know," he said, keeping his voice quiet and matter-of-fact. "I don't see how they could come from Nidor, and the Grandfathers tell us that the Earthmen do not lie. The Grandfathers have accepted the Earthmen."

"And therefore we accept them," Narla completed. The response was ritualistic.

"Of course," said Kiv.

And then the first scattered outskirts of the City of Gelusar came into sight.

II

They rode into Holy Gelusar—the city legend said was founded by the Great Light Himself. The vast, sprawling city was the center of all Nidorian culture. For two thousand and more years, it had stood almost unchanged. The city spread out radially from its center, the Great Temple, where the mighty Council of Sixteen Elders ruled the world of Nidor according to the Scripture and the Law.

Kiv and Narla guided their deests through a crowded thoroughfare that led toward the heart of the city, looking for a public communicator. They finally found one near a shabby little side street that edged off toward the river. A few black-clad sailors lounged about, evidently just having come up the Tammul river from the southerly harbor of Tammulcor. Dismounting, Kiv eyed them uneasily; coming from a line of farmers and priests, he had a deep-rooted dislike for seamen, who tended, in the main, to be a blaspheming lot.

Kiv entered. A chubby little man behind the counter took Kiv's request.

"This is a local call, then, not long distance," muttered the clerk, half to himself. "Hmmm. That will be three pieces and four."

Kiv scooped a ring of coins from his vest, unclipped several, and handed them over. He walked to the booth and closed the door. Then, picking up the microphone, he flipped the switch.

"Communications central," said a voice from the speaker.

"This is Kiv peGanz Brajjyd. I have a message for the Uncle of Public Works."

"One moment." Kiv heard a series of clicks over the speaker, and then a new voice.

"Office of Public Works. What is it, please?"

"I'm bearing a message for the Uncle from Grandfather Dom peBril Sesom at the Bridge of Klid. He asked me to tell you that he needs another squad of men if he's going to get the bridge repaired for the evening traffic."

"And your name?"

Kiv identified himself, was thanked, and cut the connection.

Outside the communications office, he found Narla talking to an elderly man—a farmer, obviously, judging by his dress.

"—and I tell you, something has to be done!" the farmer was saying. "My sons and their families are fighting desperately now, but if we run short of Edris powder, there won't be a crop this year."

"It sounds bad," Narla said. "And you say there are other farmers having the same sort of trouble?"

"Plenty of them," said the farmer. "The Great Light alone knows how many million of those damned hugl are chewing up the countryside out in my sector."

"Your pardon, Aged One," Kiv broke in, using a

term of respect even though the farmer was not really old enough to deserve the flattering term. "What's this about the hugl?"

The man turned. "They're eating my crops! They're swarming again. The swarms eat and strip everything in their path. And that goes for animals, too. They eat *everything!*"

"I realize that," Kiv said patiently. "But I hardly see that it's anything to worry about. This happens periodically, doesn't it?"

"Never like this. It seems to get worse all the time."

Kiv noticed for the first time that the farmer looked tired and travelworn. The fine golden down that covered his skin was heavy with road dust. Kiv realized suddenly that he and Narla probably looked about the same.

"I've come to talk to one of the Elder Grandfathers," the man continued. "One of my own clan, with whom I schooled as a boy. We need help out there." He took a deep breath. "May you have many children to honor you."

"And may your children and their children honor you forever," Kiv called after him as he turned and headed into the communicator office.

He remounted his deest, turned the animal's long, bony head gently, and trotted with Narla down the thoroughfare toward the Great Temple.

"He seemed worried," Narla said.

"They all do. If you'd had as much contact with farmers as I have, you'd understand. Every so often, the hugl march, and when they do, the farmers worry. Edris powder is expensive, but it's the only thing that will control the hugl. Fortunately, it *does* control them. It's a nerve poison, and it kills within a few minutes."

"The way he talked, you'd think that the hugl were

going to eat up every bit of organic matter in the whole world.''

"Remember, darling, to a farmer, his farm *is* the whole world.''

"It's almost as if the hugl wanted to destroy us,'' Narla said, her voice changing suddenly.

Kiv looked at her. "What do you mean?''

"According to the Scripture, 'To destroy a thing, one must cut at the root, and not at the branch.' And certainly, the farmer is the root of our economy.''

Kiv laughed aloud. "I see what you mean. Well, it just proves that all living things obey the Law. But I'm sure the hugl don't do it consciously.''

They rode on through the city, watching the peddlers and vendors hawking their wares. They passed by the Central Railway Terminal, where the little steam engines chuffed and puffed their way across the ancient overhead rails.

"We could have been to the School by now,'' Kiv complained. "Having to detour through the city like this is an awful waste of time.''

"What would you have done?'' Narla asked, a smile crinkling the skin around her eyes. "Swim the river where the Klid Bridge was out?''

Kiv chuckled.

"It might have been cooler at that,'' Narla went on. "I'm going to be in bad need of a bath by the time we get to the School. It's so much dustier here in the city.''

Several minutes later the Great Temple came into view. Narla glanced at Kiv and said softly, "Should we go in, Kiv?''

Kiv thought of the interior of the Temple—the vast rows of kneeling stands, the brilliant white glare of the altar, where the beams of the Great Light were focused through the huge lens in the ceiling, and the restful silence of the flickering incense candles.

But he shook his head. "No," he said. "We should have been at the School by now." Catching the little spark of petulance that flickered for a moment in Narla's eyes, he added, "We'll come back on the next Holy Day. I promise."

She nodded in silent agreement.

"That's our road," Kiv said. "Over there."

The Bel-rogas School of Divine Law was situated five miles outside the city of Gelusar, up a long, twisting turf road. They trotted out to where the road began, and started up the hill.

The Earthman Jones was a tired-looking man with faded blue eyes and a short, stiff brown beard that provided a never-ending source of conversation for the beardless Nidorians.

"Glad to see you back," he said as Narla and Kiv entered the Central Room of the School's main building, áfter having stabled their deests outside. He was sitting comfortably on a bench in one corner of the big room, leafing through a ponderous leather-bound volume.

"Have a nice visit?" Jones asked amiably. "How were the folks?"

"My parents were in good health," Kiv said. "As were Narla's."

"Good to hear it," the Earthman said. He closed his book and replaced it on a shelf just above his head. "Well? Sorry vacation's over?"

"Not at all," Kiv said. "I didn't realize how much the School meant to me until the vacation time came. All year long I was waiting impatiently for classes to end so I could go back home—"

"—But as soon as he got home he started counting the days before School started again," Narla said. "He just couldn't wait."

"Impatient, eh?" Jones said. He frowned as if considering something.

"Yes," Kiv confessed. "Impatient."

Narla said, "It's been awful, Jones. He's been ordering me around as if I were his deest. We couldn't even stop off at the Great Temple on our way through Gelusar; he was in such a hurry to get back."

"That's not true!" protested Kiv. "I did try to help repair that bridge, didn't I? And they wouldn't let me!"

"What bridge?" Jones asked.

"The Bridge of Klid. Roadbed collapsed. That's why we took the back road."

"I figured something like that must have happened. I've never seen two more bedraggled-looking people than you two. Why don't you head up to your room and get some of that dust off your skin?"

"Good idea." Kiv looked enviously at Jones' smooth skin. "You Earthmen are lucky," he said. "You have all your fur under your skin."

"A mere matter of Providence," Jones said. "For so the Great Light decreed."

"And so shall it be," Kiv completed.

"Come on," Narla said. "Let's wash up."

They started to move toward the great staircase that led up to the students' rooms. Kiv felt a warm sense of being home again when he saw the thick banister of glossy black wood.

"I suppose we're in the same room as we were last semester?"

"There's been no change in room assignment," Jones said.

"I was afraid of that," said Kiv glumly. He stared up

at the winding staircase. "That means another year of struggling up seven flights of stairs." Drawing in a resolute breath, he said, "Oh, well. So shall it be, the Scripture says. Let's go."

Kiv took Narla by one hand, hoisted his saddlebag with the other, and they started up the stairs.

When Kiv came down, half an hour later, Jones was sitting exactly where he had been before.

"You look a lot cleaner now," Jones said.

Kiv smiled broadly. "It's astonishing what a quick shower can do. But Narla's still up there scrubbing herself; her skin's glistening by now, and she still maintains she's covered with dust."

"It's been a pretty dry month. The roads are dusty."

"Don't we know it!" Kiv started to sit down, then recalled the little box that had been in his saddlebag. He clapped his hands together and dashed up the stairs, returning a few moments later with the box.

"I found this specimen on the road, when we stopped for midmeal. And forgot all about it till now, like the stupid deest I am." He handed the box to Jones.

The Earthman turned the box over and scrutinized the little animal within. The hugl still was battering the side of the box in an attempt to escape, but it had made no impression on the hard plastic.

"You notice that it's got *black* armor," Kiv pointed out.

"Oh, yes, I see that. I'm pretty well aware of what these things should look like, you know." Jones drew the box close to his eye and peered at the hugl.

"Beg pardon," Kiv said. He started to make the ritualistic bow of forgiveness, but Jones checked him with a quick gesture.

"All right, Kiv. I'm not offended." He gave the box

a quick flip; the unfortunate little prisoner went over on its back. Jones studied the creature's underside for a moment, before the hugl managed to right itself.

"What do you make of it, Jones? Why is it black? All the others are brown, you know."

"Yes, I do know," Jones said, a trifle impatiently. But before Kiv had a chance even to begin apologizing again, Jones had uncoiled himself from the bench and was walking briskly across the Central Room.

"Come with me," he said.

Kiv followed, trying to keep up with the pace set by the long-legged Earthman. "Where are we going?"

"You *have* become impatient, Kiv. Always bursting out with questions."

Kiv smiled. He recalled that not long before, he had been criticizing Narla for the same thing. Apparently he shared her fault, since he had managed to give offense to Jones three times within just a few minutes.

Had Jones been an Elder, Kiv reflected, *I'd be still finishing my ritual apology, with numbers two and three to go. It's a good thing Jones is different.*

"Here we are," Jones said. He fumbled at his waist until he managed to detach his door-opener from the belt of his shorts. He inserted it; the door clicked open.

They were in Kiv's laboratory.

"To forestall your question," Jones said, "Yes, I *have* been taking care of your pets while you were gone, as requested."

"I never doubted it," Kiv said.

"I know." Jones smiled. "Pardon me when I tease you. You're so *solemn* sometimes."

I'll never get used to the way he talks, Kiv thought. As if I were his brother, almost. And he's older than I am, by the Light! Perhaps the Earthmen will never understand that they are due the greatest respect.

Jones drew out the box containing Kiv's hugl.

"While you were gone, I started a new nest. Come here and look at it, will you?"

Kiv walked to the cabinet near the window and peered in. The cabinet swarmed with hugl, fiercely tearing what looked like the haunch of a deest to ribbons.

And every one of them was a dark, glossy black.

Kiv looked up, startled.

"They're just like mine," he said. "Black!"

"Exactly," Jones said. "Your specimen is of a type not exactly uncommon in these parts. As a matter of fact, I collected all of these on the farm of one Korvin peDrang Yorgen, not very far from here. His farm was completely overrun with them about three days ago. It should take these black hugl about ten days to reach your father's farm in—where is it—Kandor?"

Kiv stared at the Earthman's bland, unexpressive face. Suddenly, he remembered the weary old farmer Narla had encountered outside the communications office, and how he had protested so bitterly that the onslaughts of the hugl seemed to get worse every year.

"These hugl are all over the district?"

"All over," Jones said. "They go from farm to farm. Eating. They're the hungriest creatures I've ever seen. Take a look at Korvin peDrang's farm later in the day. Right out in front you'll see a very fine deest skeleton. The hugl picked it clean of flesh in less time than I can tell about it."

Kiv squinted into the cabinet again, watching the furious milling-about of the little animals. They were marching round and round their enclosure, as if mere motion would eventually free them.

"I'll testify that they're hungry beasts." He held out

his bandaged thumb for Jones' inspection. "This one I brought back took a neat chunk out of me while I was collecting him."

Jones nodded. "Oh, they'll eat anything, all right. Ask some of our farmers."

"It's funny," Kiv remarked. "Here I am, an expert on hugl, and the first time the little beasts do something significant I have to be miles away! Some specialist I am! My own animals develop a new species and begin eating deests, and I don't find out about it for days."

He stared gloomily into the big tank where his hugl larvae lived. The little teardrop-shaped animals— "water wiggles," the farmers called them—were paddling peacefully up and down in the brackish pond water Kiv had so carefully transported to his laboratory from the nearby lake where he had collected them.

"Will these be black or brown?" he asked Jones.

"How should I know? Ask them."

Kiv smiled, concealing his feeling of annoyance at the Earthman's flippancy. "I haven't learned their language," he said. "Or they haven't learned mine."

He looked back over his shoulder at Jones, who was staring out the window, watching the stream of radiance from the Great Light slowly fade from the clouded skies. It was approaching nightfall.

"I guess the poor farmers are working all day and all night to get their fields sprayed with Edris powder," Kiv said.

"They are. They've used so much that the supply is starting to run low. You can almost smell the Edris drifting on the wind, they've used so much."

"That's good. Hugl make very interesting beasts to study—but I don't feel so affectionate toward them when they threaten the crops. And it's a lucky thing the Edris powder controls them so well."

"Very lucky," said Jones. He turned to face Kiv, and there was a curious twinkle in his eyes. "But there's one other thing I haven't told you yet. The Edris powder isn't controlling these black hugl at all. Not at all."

III

Picture a multilegged little animal about half as long as your thumb. Now multiply it by a factor of between one and three million. Picture this vast horde of vicious, eternally hungry little monsters moving slowly but inexorably over the farmland of Nidor's one great continent.

Every lake and every pond could become a focal point of the infection, from which the predators would spread, consuming everything in their path.

That was the picture that sprang into Kiv's mind. If what Jones said was true, if Edris powder could no longer control the hugl, then—then—

His mind simply failed to grasp the immensity of the disaster. So he rejected it. He shook his head, partly in negation, partly to clear it.

"That doesn't seem right," he said uneasily. "Edris powder will kill hugl. It's *always* killed them. For thousands of years. Why shouldn't it kill them now? What difference does their color make?"

The last glow of the Great Light streamed through the

47

window and outlined Jones' head. The Earthman's face
was coolly expressionless.

"That's what you ought to find out, isn't it?"

"But—but Jones—how do you know Edris powder
won't kill them?"

"The same way you would have found out if you'd
been here when the first ones appeared." The Earthman
stopped, his alien eyes looking at Kiv's own.

Kiv met the Earthman's glance, as he tried to penetrate the peculiar logic of Jones' thought processes.

"If I'd caught one, I'd have tried to dissect it, I
suppose. Naturally, I'd have killed it first. But I'd have
used the gas generator. I don't understand."

Jones smiled. "That's because I withheld a minor bit
of information. The gas generator overheated several
weeks ago and cracked."

Kiv nodded. "So you used Edris instead. And—it
didn't work?"

Frowning, the Earthman said, "I wouldn't say it
didn't work altogether. The thing finally died, but it
took a rather long time. Four days."

"*Four days?*" Kiv's voice held a touch of awe. The
long shadows began to gather in the little laboratory
room, and he reached for the illuminator cord. "Four
days?" He paused, holding the cord, letting the implications of Jones' statement sink in.

There was a diffident knock on the door. Narla
stepped inside.

"I thought I'd find you here." She looked around.
"What are you two so somber about? Look."

She held out a small printed booklet. "According to
the Term Bulletin, I'm eligible to take Grandfather
Syg's course—Application of Canon Law. Didn't you
say you were going to take it, Kiv?"

"I wouldn't miss it for anything," Kiv said, glad to

get his mind off the peculiarities of the black hugl for a moment.

"Grandfather Syg is a brilliant man," Jones said in his soft voice. "I believe McKay is working with him on teaching technique." Abruptly, Jones rose. "You'll have to excuse me now," he said.

After Jones had left the lab, Kiv turned to look again at the peacefully-swimming hugl larvae. "I don't think I'll ever understand these Earthmen," he said.

"Nor will I," Narla agreed. "But you'll have to admit that the School has done some wonderful things for Nidor."

"Yes," Kiv said absently.

"Their new teaching techniques enable us to learn faster and remember more. We can understand the Law and the Scriptures much better than any of our Ancestors did."

Kiv hardly heard her. He continued to stare at the larva tank. Then the meaning of her words reached him, and he saw that she was implying criticism of the Ancestors. And that, to Kiv's tradition-heavy mind, was not far from sacrilege.

"Narla!"

"I'm sorry," she said quickly. "I didn't mean to say anything disrespectful. I guess I'll never understand."

And then he had to console her.

Before another day had passed, all the students of the Bel-rogas School had returned. The spacious green parks that surrounded the cluster of buildings were soon filled with young men and women, and the soft hum of their conversation carried through the air.

But their talk now vibrated with strange undertones. Several of them from the northern province of Sugon had not shown up at all. Rumor had it that they were fighting to save their parents' farms from the onslaught of the armies of hugl.

And Kiv didn't like it.

"There should be *something* we can do about it," he exclaimed to Narla. "There must be some way of stopping them."

"Edris powder," Narla said. "Edris powder kills the hugl. Edris powder has always killed the hugl."

"But it's not killing them now," Kiv said savagely, and sank back into his gloom. The new semester was sliding by, and only one thing obsessed him: the failure of the Edris powder.

The Scripture prescribed Edris powder. Not in so many words, perhaps. But it did say, "Those ways are best which have been tried and pass the test."

Edris powder had passed the test. As long as there had been hugl, the Edris powder had controlled them.

But now the powder was failing. Could the test be passed once and then failed, Kiv wondered?

And more important: *could the Scripture be wrong?*

The thought sickened him.

The first three days of the new semester made little impression on him. He studied, but only half-heartedly, and what he learned left him as soon as classes ended. On the fourth day, eight of the young men Kiv knew asked permission to leave. They had received word that they were needed at home.

Within a week, the hugl problem had grown from a nuisance to the status of a full-fledged menace.

"You're not studying," Narla said, as Kiv stared uneasily at the page of his textbook. "You're looking, but you're not studying. What's the matter?"

"Nothing," he said, and tried to focus his attention. But he was unable to study. He rubbed the palm of his hand over the light golden hair that blurred the outlines of his face, and shifted worriedly in his seat. He felt nervous without quite knowing what he was nervous about. The destruction of acres of crops, and even the occasional reports of lives being lost, bothered him—but he knew it was something else, something deeper and subtler, that gnawed at the back of his mind.

I'll look at it as if I'm an Earthman, he told himself. *The Scripture says, Rely on trusted things. The Scripture itself is a trusted thing. For thousands of years it has guided us safely. We are happy, contented with our world and its ways.*

But what happens when the trusted guide no longer leads in the right direction? For a moment, Kiv pretended that he was Jones, and tried to look at the situation through the alien eyes of an Earthman.

When the trusted guide no longer leads, Jones might say—what?

Get a new guide?

He sat down to think it through—the whole thing, still using Jones' mind as a focus. And when he came up with what he thought was a conclusion, he went somewhat timidly to Jones.

He explained his thought.

"I don't quite see what you mean, Kiv," the Earthman said, his eyes inscrutable. He leaned back in the comfortable chair, facing Kiv in the tiny cubicle that was Jones' office.

"Well, look here: we know that Edris powder is a nerve poison, right?"

Jones nodded wordlessly.

"Well, then, why doesn't it kill this new kind of hugl? I thought about it a long time, and I finally came up with an answer—at least, I *think* it's an answer." Kiv looked at Jones for reassurance; the Earthman seemed somehow to smile with his eyes.

"Edris kills through the epidermis of the animal," Kiv went on. "It doesn't bother them if they eat it. Now: if a nerve poison doesn't work, it's because it's not getting to the nerves. I checked my theory by measuring the thickness of the chitin armor of these black hugl, and I came up with something odd: the armor is half again as thick and considerably denser than the armor of the normal animal. The Edris takes longer to penetrate, and it takes more of it. That's my guess. How does it sound to you?"

Jones rubbed his smooth fingers through his chin hair. "It sounds perfectly logical to me. What about it?"

"Well, then, if we kill them when they're still in the larval stage, they won't have the protection armor. Edris can be put in the lakes and ponds in quantities great enough to kill the larval hugl without endangering any other aquatic life."

"Perhaps," Jones said.

"I'm sure of it," returned Kiv, just a little surprised at his own new confidence. "I'd like to go down to Gelusar to see the Council of Elders. If they'll send the word out over the wires in time, we can stop the hugl onslaught before it gets any further and becomes really serious. If you would come with me to Gelusar, we could explain how this might work, and—"

He stopped. He could read the expression on the Earthman's face clearly, and he knew what it meant.

Jones confirmed it.

"I'm sorry, Kiv. We're here only to teach, not to interfere in government policies. If you want to go to the Council, you certainly have my permission to do so. In fact, you don't even need my permission." Jones smiled. "It is said in the Scripture: 'You shall govern yourselves according to the Law.' " He accented the *yourselves*.

Kiv considered that for a moment. "All right," he said. "You've got me there. But it's not fair."

"The Scripture is a potent arguing force, Kiv. Don't ever forget that." The Earthman's pale blue eyes looked steadily at him. "If you can understand and use the Scripture and the Law, you need fear nothing— neither here, nor in the sky."

"I—I see. Very well, Jones. If you think it's the right way, I'll go to the Council alone."

Kiv left the room without another word. His thoughts were confused, not angry. Somehow, the Earthmen always seemed to strike at the very root of a problem, no matter how complex.

And they could back up their solutions with unerring reference to the unanswerable Scripture.

Kiv turned his thoughts over in his mind as his deest trotted down the winding road to the Holy City.

Gelusar, located centrally on Nidor in the heart of the Province of Dimay, perched on the river Tammul and thus was both the religious and commercial center of the nation. In the heart of all loomed the Great Temple.

Kiv had brought his notebooks and his specimen drawings with him; they would constitute his argument in favor of the new plan. He would have to be absolutely sure of what he was saying before he would be able to convince the all-powerful Council of Elders.

He had plenty of time. Because of the press of the emergency, it took four days to gain an audience with the Elder of his Clan.

Kiv spent the four days wandering the city, trying not to worry. Narla came down from the School to join him on the second day, and they passed most of their time in

the Great Temple, staring at the huge lens through
which the Great Light was focused.

Finally, notification came through that Grandfather
Bor peDrogh Brajjyd would see him.

Theoretically, any of the Elders of the Council of
Sixteen would have done—but in practice it was customary to call upon one's own Clan Elder. As a member
of the Clan Brajjyd, Kiv was obliged to seek audience
with Grandfather Bor peDrogh Brajjyd.

And Grandfather Bor peDrogh had been extremely
busy for the past three days. On the fourth day, however, he consented to see Kiv; because of the young
man's status in the Bel-rogas School, the audience was
to last for a full half hour.

A short, dark-hued young acolyte, also of the Clan
Brajjyd, ushered Kiv in. The Elder Grandfather's office
was not ornate, but neither was it austere. It was deco-
rated in simple good taste, with the customary sym-
bol of the Great Light in its honored niche in the
wall.

The Elder Grandfather's extreme age was evident in
every line of his body. The golden aura of body hair had
long since turned to silver, and was growing sparse on
his face, making him look oddly like an Earthman. His
face was lined but peaceful, and his hands, though
gnarled with age, were still quick and graceful.

Kiv knelt and bowed his head.

"The peace of your Ancestors be with you always,"
said the priest. His voice was deeper and more virile
than Kiv had expected.

"And may the Great Light illumine your mind as He
does the world," Kiv responded.

"Sit down, my son." The old man's bass voice again
startled Kiv. "Tell me what it is that troubles you."

"It's the hugl, Grandfather. The farmers are having a
terrible time controlling them, and I understand the

situation has been getting worse for the past six days.''

"This is correct. But just what is it you wish to tell me?"

Kiv drew a deep breath. The Grandfather suddenly seemed terribly, terribly ancient. For a wild moment Kiv thought of throwing himself at the old man's feet to beg forgiveness for—

No, he told himself. *Pretend you are Jones*.

The Grandfather was awaiting his reply with patience. Kiv said, "I think I've found something that might help, Grandfather. To wipe out the hugl, that is.''

The shadow of a frown passed across the wrinkled face. "I see. Go on, my son." Still not a trace of impatience on the part of the Grandfather.

Kiv pulled his charts and drawings out of a leather carrying case.

"The trouble is," he began, "that not very much is known about the hugl. Up to now, the Edris powder has controlled them well, so there was, of course, no reason to study them. But I did it as a sort of—well, as a sort of hobby, Grandfather. We call them 'projects' at the School: some little facet of life that we choose to study in order to gain greater illumination in the Great Light's Law.''

"I have heard that the Earthmen have ingenious ways of helping youngsters to learn," said the old man. "I think it's commendable. Very. And so you studied the hugl?''

"Yes, Grandfather. And I found out some rather weird things. You know those little teardrop-shaped things that you see swimming in ponds and lakes—the little animals that farmers call 'water wiggles'? Well, these are *young* hugl!''

"Young hugl?" The Grandfather frowned. "But they look nothing like hugl.''

"I know, Grandfather," Kiv said. "That's the amazing thing. The young start out as little 'water wiggles' and live that way for most of their lives—about a year. They eat soft water plants and decaying organic matter, since they have no teeth.

"After a year of this kind of life, they go down to the bottom and bury themselves in the mud, where they stay for thirty-five to forty days. During that time, they live in a sort of shell built out of mud. They absorb their endoskeletons and grow exoskeletons. When they emerge, they're hugl. The hugl," Kiv concluded triumphantly, "is the adult female form of the water wiggle.

"As soon as it cracks out of its shell in the mud, the adult hugl goes to the surface and swims to land. As I said, the thing we call the hugl is the female; the male is a much smaller animal, hardly more than an animated sex organ.

"The mating takes place on land, and the female immediately eats the male. Then she goes out and looks for more food—anything she can eat. And as long as she finds nothing to eat, she'll keep going looking for more—until she starves to death.

"If she does find food, she eats all she can hold, converting it into a kind of predigested concentrate. But her system can't assimilate anything she eats; her body just stores it.

"When she's eaten enough—when her glands tell her she's at the proper point—she crawls to a lake or pond, dies, and drops to the bottom.

"The eggs are never laid; they remain within the body of the female. The dead female, protected from dissolution by her hard armor, provides food for the young larvae for the first few days of their life, until they're ready to go out and hunt for food of their own.

Then the cycle begins all over again,'' Kiv concluded.

The old priest had looked carefully at Kiv's diagrams and had seemed to be following his lecture with interest. When Kiv had finished, the Grandfather rose and wandered to the window overlooking the Square of Holy Light. He nodded slowly.

''Very interesting. Very! And what bearing does this have on our present crisis, now?''

''I'm coming to that, Grandfather. You see, the reason that Edris powder isn't working so well this time is simply that a new variety of hugl has appeared which has an exoskeleton too heavy and dense to allow the Edris powder to penetrate very rapidly.''

''A *new* variety?'' He sounded skeptical.

''And if we put the powder in the ponds,'' Kiv said, ''it will kill the young; their skins will absorb it immediately.''

Kiv sat back expectantly. The old man returned to his desk, sat down, and began toying with a heavy, jewel-encrusted paper-weight. Finally the Grandfather said:

''A very interesting theory, and very ingeniously worked out. But I'm afraid it's not really of much practical use. As the Scripture says, 'Those ways are best which have been tried and passed the test.' ''

I might have known that was coming, Kiv thought.

''You see,'' said the priest, ''we have already alleviated the problem very simply. The farmers haven't been using enough of the Edris powder to cope with these hugl. Since the menace has been largely confined to the north so far, we have simply shipped additional quantities of Edris to the northern farmers. The hugl are dying.''

''I see,'' Kiv said softly.

The Grandfather rose in what could only be a gesture of dismissal. ''I'm happy you told me all about the hug1, my son. Your instructors at the School must be fine ones. And now, I have another appointment. May the blessings of the Great Light beam down upon you and your children.''

IV

"—and, of course, he was right," Kiv told Jones. "And I can understand why you wanted no part of it."

"You can, eh?" The Earthman's eyes were glittering oddly. "Kiv, have you thought about what's going to happen in the next thirty days? The hugl are swarming down out of the north; they'll be maturing in the south soon, and then there'll be trouble." Pausing, Jones jabbed a forefinger at Kiv. "If the Council diverts the south's supplies of Edris to the north, what's going to happen?" he demanded.

"I don't know," Kiv said, scratching his fuzzy head in puzzlement, "I really don't know."

Jones stood up and walked toward the door of Kiv's room. "Yes, you do. You're just afraid to say it out loud."

Kiv picked up a book and weighed it idly with one hand. He had to admit that as usual Jones had cut right to the heart of the problem.

"All right. If things keep on like this, either the south

or the north or both will be wiped clean of crops in a hurry.''

Jones nodded in solemn agreement. ''A fine situation, don't you think?''

Before Kiv could reply, the Earthman had walked through the door and was gone.

Classes continued as usual in Bel-rogas, but over everything hung an invisible cloud of fear and uncertainty. Kiv found himself far too preoccupied with the crisis to be able to devote much time to his studies, and he couldn't even bear the thought of working in his laboratory. The sight of hugl had become completely abhorrent to him.

And then the reports began to trickle down from the north.

The Edris powder, when used in large enough amounts, killed even the black hugl quite nicely. Unfortunately, it was also killing the crops. The peych plants, staple crop of Nidor, withered and shrivelled under the poison.

Stalemate. Either let the hugl eat the peych crops, or kill the peych before harvest time with an excess of Edris powder.

''In either case, people are going to go hungry,'' Kiv told Narla.

''I suppose they'll begin rationing soon.''

Kiv didn't even bother to reply.

''Kiv?''

He turned to look up at Narla. Her face seemed thin already, he thought. *Perhaps it's only my imagination. There isn't any famine yet. Not yet.*

''What is it?'' he asked wearily.

''Kiv, didn't the Grandfather want to listen at all when you went to him?''

''I told you. He listened very carefully. He just

wasn't open to suggestions, that's all. The Way of the Ancestors was going to provide the answer, he said. It was all very simple. He—''

He broke off.

Kiv studied the golden-fuzzed backs of his hands and said no more. The implications now were terrifying to him. The Grandfathers were following the Scripture, and starvation was the consequence.

But yet the Great Light still streamed through the window.

"I'll go to Jones," Kiv said in a troubled voice. "Jones will help me."

Jones looked up quizzically when Kiv entered the tiny office.

"I hope I didn't disturb your work—" Kiv began apologetically.

Jones put him at ease immediately with a quick grin. "Of course not. What's on your mind, Kiv?"

Kiv sat down in the deep chair that faced the Earthman. Nervously he fumbled for an opening.

"The hugl?" Jones prompted.

"If they'd only accepted my plan!" Kiv broke out, almost bitterly. "Now what will they do?"

Jones leaned forward, and Kiv felt a sudden glow of confidence radiating from the Earthman. The thought struck him that there could be no doubt that the Earthmen must really be from the Great Light; in their quiet, inconspicuous way, they had become the props on which the Nidorians could lean in time of trouble.

When the Earthmen arrived, Kiv thought, *they said they were here to guide us toward the Light. So my father Ganz told me. And it must be true.*

"What will they do now?" Kiv repeated, wondering if Jones knew the answer.

And Jones did. "Kiv," the Earthman said softly, "You just didn't approach the Grandfather the right way. You didn't show him how the situation was according to the Law."

"How could I?" Kiv burst out. "There's nothing in the Law about this!"

Jones held up a hand. "You're still too impatient, Kiv. Listen to me. For one thing, you didn't tell him that you had watched the life cycle of the hugl with your own eyes. The Elder Grandfather probably thought you were just speculating. But if you could offer some scriptural passage that would—"

Suddenly Kiv smiled. "I've got it! It was a passage that Narla quoted, from the Fourteenth Section: 'To destroy a thing, one must cut at the root, and not at the branch.'

"Jones! I'm going back to Gelusar!"

The dark-hued little acolyte attempted to block Kiv as he burst into the vestibule of Elder Grandfather Bor peDrogh Brajjyd's office.

"You can't go in there like that!" the acolyte said.

"This is important," Kiv snapped.

"I say you can't go in there. The Elder Grandfather's not there, anyway."

"Where is he?"

"He's at a meeting of the Council," the acolyte said. "Not that that could possibly concern *you.*"

Kiv didn't stay to argue the point. He dashed down the corridor and sped across the crowded street to the dome of the Great Temple.

Then, almost unthinkingly, he plunged inside and found himself heading toward the High Councilroom. The enormity of what he was doing did not strike him until he was inside the ornate room, facing the sixteen Elder Grandfathers as they sat in a majestic semi-circle.

They didn't even notice him for a while, so intent were they on their deliberations. Kiv glanced from one to another. There was the Elder of the Clan Sesom—Narla's Clan. He recognized several of the other Clan Elders among the venerable assemblage. The very tall, gaunt man was Yorgen peYorgen Yorgen, a lineal descendant of the great Bel-rogas. Everyone knew him. And the somewhat plump Elder in crimson robes was Ganz peDrang Kovnish. Next to him, Kiv recognized the familiar face of the Elder Brajjyd whom he had seen earlier. The others Kiv did not know.

Finally one of the Elders noticed him.

"What are you doing here? Who are you?"

Kiv felt a desire to turn and run. He held his ground, however, when he saw the Elder Brajjyd smiling at him.

"This man is of my Clan," Elder Grandfather said in his prodigious bass rumble. "He spoke to me before; he has studied the hugl at Bel-rogas."

At the mention of the School's name Kiv perceived a visible change in the manner of the Council.

"He had some interesting information for me. But what is it you want now?" The Elder Grandfather leaned forward as if to hear Kiv's reply more clearly.

Slowly, as if there were no one in the room but some other students at the School, Kiv began to explain the life-cycle of the hugl to the Council as he had to the Elder Brajjyd. They watched with apparent interest as he spoke.

When he finished, it was the Elder Kovnish who broke the silence first.

"The Scripture says on this matter that—"

Had it been the fierce-looking Elder Yorgen who was speaking, Kiv would have never dared interrupt. But the chubby Elder Kovnish did not seem so terrifying to Kiv. He cut the Elder off in mid-sentence.

"Yes—the Scripture." Kiv cited Narla's quotation: "To destroy a thing, cut at the root, not at the branch."

"Fourteenth Section," the Elder Yorgen said in a sepulchral voice.

And then it seemed to Kiv that he was talking to the Elders as if they might be pupils of his. Heatedly he threw out his arms.

"Don't you see? The branch means the adult hugl; the root means the larva! It's right there in the Scripture: cut at the root of the menace! Pour Edris powder into the lakes; kill the larvae!"

The sixteen members of the Council stared coldly at Kiv for what seemed to him an infinitely long time. Then, as the meaning of his demonstration broke through to them, their stony silence became an excited hubbub.

"That's the last of it," said Nibro peGanz Kovnish. The burly farmer crumpled the empty packet of Edris powder and let it fall to the ground. He turned to face Kiv, who stood watching him.

"Craziest thing I ever heard," Nibro peGanz said. "Dumping Edris into my lake. Might as well lie down and let the hugl eat me too."

"Patience, friend. The Council has decided."

"And therefore I accept," the farmer responded reluctantly.

"Right. I'll be back to check on your farm in six days."

Kiv mounted his deest and trotted on down to the next farm. He had much ground to cover.

The six days passed slowly, and then Kiv revisited the farms in the test areas.

The few hugl that had made their appearance didn't even constitute a swarm, much less a menace.

"It's all over," he said, throwing open the door of Jones' office with an assurance he had never known before. The Earthman was waiting inside, with Narla.

"What happened?" Narla asked anxiously.

"As expected. Perfectly as expected. Hardly a hugl to be found."

Narla sighed in relief; Jones' face creased in a broad smile.

"Congratulations," the Earthman said. "I guess that makes you a celebrity. The Man Who Saved the World."

"It was your doing, Jones. You showed me how."

Jones shook his head. "Ah, no! It was *your* doing. I'm merely here as a guide. My aim is eventually to bring you and your people to the Great Light, Kiv. But actually I will only help you to bring yourselves. When you guide a deest, it is still the deest, not you, who is doing the real work."

Kiv frowned. "I don't care much for your analogy."

"Don't let him upset you," Narla said. "He's only teasing again." She drew close to him. "I'm tremendously proud of you."

Jones rubbed his beard with a forefinger. "In a way, Kiv, I am too. I can't help but think of how much you've learned since you came to Bel-rogas. You've really made progress."

"Do you think he should become a priest? And maybe someday become an Elder?" Narla asked.

"Why, I think they ought to put him on the Council

right away," Jones said, smiling. "After all, if he's capable of walking right in there and telling the Council how to run Nidor—"

Jones paused and stared meaningfully at Kiv. Kiv met his glance with difficulty. There was something strange in the Earthman's blue eyes.

"Let's go outside," Kiv said. "The air in here's none too fresh."

At the suggestion, Narla and Jones arose. The three of them filed out of Jones' office.

Kiv considered what Jones had just said during the passage down the stairs. *After all, if he's capable of walking right in and telling the Council how to run Nidor—*

But they were *Elders*, and he was only Kiv peGanz Brajjyd, an insignificant student. And he had told them what to do. And they had accepted it.

The thought cut suddenly deep into him. Since the beginning of time, young men had sat quietly and listened to the counsels of the Elders. Now, barely more than two cycles after the Earthmen had descended from the sky, the age-old pattern had begun to break.

Was this the way the Earthmen were leading them toward the Light?

The enormity of what Kiv had done struck him, and then the even greater enormity that no one had questioned his action. No one. The Earthmen's stay was having its effect on Nidor, all right.

They reached the foot of the stairs. Absently, Kiv turned to enter the little room where his laboratory was. He opened the door and saw the rows and rows of cabinets, each with their specimens of hugl, and right in the center of the room was the larva tank.

"Where are you going, Kiv?" Jones called. "I thought you wanted some fresh air."

Jones began to walk through the front door, followed by Narla. Kiv hastened to catch up with them.

Turning as Kiv reached the door, Jones asked, "What's on your mind, Kiv peGanz?"

"Nothing, Jones. Nothing." But he was certain the Earthman knew exactly what *was* on his mind.

He stepped out of the building onto the front lawn of the Bel-rogas campus. He looked up, and the Great Light illumined the cloud-laden sky. Suddenly Kiv thought again of the quotation from the Fourteenth Section—and for some reason, his head began to hurt.

243rd CYCLE

I

Time passed; the Year of Danoy of the 243rd Cycle swung round, and the hugl died away. And the name of Kiv peGanz Brajjyd became an important one at the Bel-rogas School of Divine Law.

Tradition-minded, Kiv was plagued by the implications of the method he had used to bring about the end of the hugl plague. But Jones speedily convinced him that the means were justified by the ends; the peych crop had been saved, and the Scripture upheld.

Throughout Nidor, the Bel-rogas School was hailed for having produced such a one as Kiv. "An obvious choice for the Council of Elders some day," people said. It put a sort of aura over Kiv: his accomplishment had marked him out as a future Elder, when his time came.

Only the manufacturers of the Edris powder suffered, and that did not make itself felt until the following year. The hugl were all but exterminated—and those whose family livelihoods had depended, for thousands of years, on manufacturing Edris powder to stem the plagues of the little beasts, now had no niche to fill in the well-balanced Nidorian economy.

Kiv brooded over that, knowing that it was his fault this had come about, as the poverty-stricken Edris manufacturers flooded into Gelusar to lay their grievances before the Council of Elders.

"I did that," he said in bitter self-accusation to Narla. "I broke the pattern, and now look!"

Narla iKiv let her hands rest lightly on her husband's shoulders. "There had to be suffering, one way or another. Either the Edris manufacturers lost out, or all Nidor would have been stripped by the hugl. Which would you prefer, Kiv?"

He thought that over for a while. "I did right, then," he said at length. "But still—nothing like this had ever happened, before. The necessity for such a choice was—"

Shaking his head, he let the conversation die. Already he was learning to hide his deepest woe within himself—and, as time went on, he became more and more convinced that he had done the only thing that had been possible for him to do. It was small comfort, but it sufficed.

He pursued his studies through the following year, dwelling mainly on aspects of theological law. Marked as he was for future acclaim, he knew he had to prepare himself diligently and well for the responsibilities that lay ahead.

He and Narla graduated from Bel-rogas a year later, the Year Lokness of the 243rd Cycle: Kiv with honors, Narla merely with an honorary commendation. But that suited Narla. She had never been an outstanding student, and in any event no possible future lay ahead for her except that which she had already chosen for herself.

On the eleventh day after graduation, she presented Kiv with a daughter.

They named her Sindi geKiv Brajjyd.

To no one's surprise, Kiv was tapped for the priesthood and selected for service at the Great Temple. He and Narla settled of necessity in Gelusar, taking a small apartment almost in the shadow of the Temple.

He had grown up in the sprawling farmlands of Thyvash, far to the southeast, and he would have preferred that his daughter have the same sort of childhood. But Temple service demanded his constant presence in the Holy City, and so city life was imposed on him.

The years passed.

The newly-designated Grandfather Kiv took a post on the staff of Drel peNibro Brajjyd, one of the ranking priests—and, when the incumbent Elder Brajjyd, old Bor peDrogh, died, it was Grandfather Drel peNibro who succeeded to the Council post.

Kiv served as the new Elder Grandfather's second-in-command, and—the memory of his great achievement still bright—was generally regarded as the heir apparent to the Council seat, some day when he had achieved the requisite standing of age in his Clan.

So the years slipped by: Sindi grew out of childhood, becoming first a gawky young girl, then, much to Kiv's amused surprise, almost a woman. He was unhappy, though; city life had made something of Sindi that hurt and displeased him.

Seeds of rebellion seemed to sprout in her. She said and did things that in the old days would have resulted in her instant punishment—but no longer.

The world was changing, Kiv realized sadly, as he grew older.

But he was proud of his daughter, nonetheless. Her impudence was just one facet of her inquisitive mind, a feature he liked to think she had inherited from him. And she followed the ways of her father in at least one respect: she applied for admission to the Bel-rogas School when she was of the proper age.

Naturally, she was accepted—naturally, both because of her father's great reputation and because of her own quick wits. In the Year of Nitha of the 244th Cycle, just twenty-one years after Kiv peGanz Brajjyd had quelled the hugl plague, Sindi, his daughter, was enrolled as a student at the Bel-rogas School of Divine Law.

SINDI

I

They were having something of a ceremony. Out on the lawn in front of the main building of the Bel rogas School of Divine Law, they were celebrating the School's anniversary. On this date, sixty-one years before, the Earthmen had come down from the sky to help bring the Law to the people of Nidor. Elder Grandfather Kinis peCharnok Yorgen had officiated at the dedication of the ground; the Earthman Jones had descended from the sky in a shining ship.

Sindi geKiv Brajjyd, who was in her first year of study at the School, stood in the shadows of the stable behind the great building and watched the multitude out front. All she could think of was the way they were crushing the grass on the lawn. It seemed a silly and overly sentimental thing to her, all this speech-making.

She patted the smooth flank of her deest. "There, boy," she said soothingly. "I'm bored too."

The graceful animal snorted and nosed up against the

hitching post as if he were anxious to be almost any-where but where he was.

That was the way Sindi felt too, she decided, as her sharp eyes picked out the earnest face of her father. He was seated out front. Kiv, like a good alumnus and responsible leader of Nidorian society, had, of course, come to Bel-rogas to take in the festivities. Right now he was watching the speaker as if he were the Great Light Himself.

As a matter of fact, the speaker actually was Grand-father Drel peNibro Brajjyd, the current Brajjyd rep-resentative on the Council of Elders. Grandfather Drel peNibro had succeeded to the ruling body some ten years earlier, on the death of the venerable Bor pe-Drogh Brajjyd. Sindi was still able to remember the gnarled, silvered old man who had headed their clan in the years before the accession of Drel peNibro.

She had seen Grandfather Bor peDrogh preside over the Feast of the Sixteen Clans only a few weeks before his death. That had been when she was seven.

Grandfather Drel peNibro was a pompous, some-what self-important old man who loved making speeches at ceremonial occasions. Sindi was aware of her father's private opinion of him—that he was a tradition-bound, unintelligent old man who had suc-ceeded to the Council solely because he had outlasted all the deserving contenders.

Kiv, who was a priest in Drel peNibro's entourage, had let that opinion drop once in Sindi's hearing, and had done his best to cover for it. But Sindi had noticed it, and it formed part of her mental approach toward the Nidorian Grandfatherhood that constituted the Council.

Sindi watched Drel peNibro from the shelter of the deest-stable. He was wearing the full formal regalia of a Council member, a flamboyant outfit which seemed to

Sindi a fairly silly affair and yet somehow still terribly impressive. His voice floated to her through the quiet air of the Nidorian mid-afternoon.

". . . this noble day . . ." he was saying, and then his voice drifted out of the range of her hearing. In the distance Sindi heard the chuffing of the Central Railway Extension that ran the five miles from the Holy City of Gelusar to the Bel-rogas School.

Then his voice became audible again. Sindi managed to catch his words as he said, ". . . is our duty to express gratitude toward our benefactors. And yet we cannot do it directly. For whatever benefits the Earthmen have brought us, these sixty-one years, are creditable, not to them—let me make that clear, not to them—but to the Agent of their arrival on our soil."

The Elder Grandfather looked upward. The multitude assembled followed suit, and Sindi found herself doing the same. She stared at the iron-gray cloud layer which partially obscured the Great Light without hiding His effulgence completely from view.

Then Grandfather Drel peNibro went on. "The Bel-rogas School, in its sixty-one years of bringing the Law to the young people of Nidor, has served as an incalculably valuable—"

Sindi strained to catch the Elder's words, which were competing with the harsh breathing-sounds of the deest and the distant drone of the railway. As she leaned forward to hear better—because, though she was too independent a girl to take part willingly in any such foolishness as the anniversary ceremony, she was far too curious about everything to let a word of it escape her ears—as she leaned forward, a new voice came from directly behind her, startling her.

"Sindi? What are you doing here?"

She whirled and saw a tall, grave-looking man dismounting from a deest and reaching for a hitching-rope. He was pale-skinned, dark-eyed, and bearded—the Earthman, Smith.

"Hello," Sindi said, uncertainly.

Smith drew a cloth from his pocket and wiped his face. He was sweating heavily, as most of the Earthmen did in Nidor's moist air. Sindi saw that his deest was near the point of exhaustion. Obviously, Smith had had a long, hard ride from somewhere.

"Why aren't you out there listening to the Grandfather?" Smith asked. His voice was kind and gentle, like those of all the other Earthmen. "All of the students belong out there, you know. You should be with them."

Sindi nodded absently. "My father's out there too," she said.

Suddenly Smith moved very close to her, and she became conscious of his curious Earthman odor. His eyes were weary-looking; his beard needed combing. He looked at her for a long time without speaking.

"Tell me," he finally said. "*Why* aren't you out there with everyone else? Why aren't you with them?"

Sindi slowly rubbed her hand back and forth over her deest's flank. "Because," she said thoughtfully, not wanting to get into any additional trouble. "Just—because."

"That's not enough of a reason."

Suddenly Sindi felt terribly small and young. "It bored me," she said. "I just didn't want to have to sit out there all day and listen to—" she paused, horrified at herself.

"—and listen to the Elder Brajjyd," Smith completed. He smiled. "Ah, Sindi, how your father would like to hear you say that!"

She shot a panicky glance at him. "You wouldn't tell

him, would you? I didn't mean anything by it! Smith—Smith—''

"Don't worry." He reached out and patted her shoulder, caressing the soft golden fuzz that covered it. "Suppose you go over now and take part in the rest of the ceremony, and let me worry about keeping secrets."

"Thanks, Smith," she said, all fear gone. "I'll go out and hear what the Elder has to say, I guess." She thumped her deest fondly, smiled at the Earthman, and walked toward the crowd.

Very carefully she tiptoed across the lawn and melted into the audience. The Elder Brajjyd was still speaking. His powerful voice rang out clearly and well.

"You see the products of this school around you," the Elder said. "The most valuable members of our priesthood; the leaders of our society; our most brilliant minds—we may trace them all to the Bel-rogas School of Divine Law. I regret," said the Elder sadly, "that I, myself, was unable to attend the School. But before many years elapse, I think it is fairly safe to say, the Council of Elders will be constituted almost totally of graduates of the Bel-rogas School.

"I see among you today, in this very gathering, men who will undoubtedly hold Council seats one day. From my own clan alone I see several—there is that brilliant Bel-rogas alumnus, Grandfather Kiv peGanz Brajjyd, now one of the most valued members of my staff, and there are others here as well. And to whom do we owe this? To whom—''

The Elder's voice grew louder and more impassioned.

Sindi threaded her way through the close-packed listeners searching for her father. She tried to remember where he had been sitting when she saw him from the stable, and headed in that general direction. The assembled Nidorians were sitting quietly and soaking in the Elder's words. He launched into a long quotation from the Scripture, which Sindi, almost as a reflex, recognized as being from the Eighteenth Section. As the Elder began to unfold the complexities of the quotation, Sindi caught sight of Kiv again. There was an empty seat at his left. No doubt she had been expected to be sitting there.

She edged through the narrow aisle and slid into the seat. Kiv nodded a rather cold welcome to her as she sat down.

"Thus, as it is said in the Scripture," the Elder went on, " 'Those beloved of the Great Light shall hold tomorrow in their hands.' We must never forget this, my friends. May the Great Light illumine your minds as He does the world."

Drel peNibro stepped down from the rostrum and took his seat. The assembly relaxed, easing the long tension built up while the Elder was speaking. Kiv leaned over to whisper to Sindi.

"Where have you been?" he asked harshly. "I've been expecting you all afternoon. You said you'd meet me for midmeal!"

"I'm sorry, Kiv," she told him. "I was busy in the labs and couldn't get free till just now."

"In the labs? On Commemoration Day? Sindi, if you're—"

"Please, Kiv", she said in annoyance. "I came as quickly as I could. Have I missed much?"

"Only the Elder Brajjyd's speech," Kiv said in a tone of heavy sarcasm. "He mentioned me. Apparently I'm back in his good graces for a while, no thanks to you."

"*Father!* You know I didn't mean to seem disre-

spectful, that day I didn't give the Grandfather the
proper salute. It was only that I was late for classes,
and—''

"Forget it, Sindi. The Elder seemed quite upset
about it at the time, but perhaps he's forgotten it.
Meanwhile, I've brought someone I'd like you to
meet."

Kiv gestured to a strange man sitting at his left.
"This is Yorgen peBor Yorgen," Kiv said. "Yorgen
peBor, this is my daughter, Sindi geKiv."

"Pleased, I'm sure," Yorgen peBor said, in a not-
very-enthusiastic tone. Sindi returned his greeting with
a similar sentiment.

"You may know Yorgen peBor's father," Kiv continued. "The Grandfather Bor peYorgen Yorgen. And
you're aware who *his* father is, aren't you?"

Kiv's tone of voice left little doubt.

"The Elder Grandfather Yorgen peYorgen Yorgen,
of course."

"Yorgen peBor here is his son's son. I'd—I'd like
you two to get to know each other well, Sindi." Kiv
smiled. What was on his mind was perfectly plain.

Rahn, Sindi thought, half-despairingly. *Rahn—I
won't forget you, anyway.*

"Certainly, Father," she said aloud, concealing her
distress. "I'm sure Yorgen peBor and I will get along
splendidly together."

"I'm sure also," Kiv said. He gestured toward the
speaker's platform. "That's not Grandfather Syg going
up there to speak, is it? Why, he was teaching here
when *I* was going to the School!"

"That's who it is, none the less," Sindi said.

She watched the aged figure climb painfully to the
rostrum. The old man, speaking in a dry, withered
voice, made some rambling prefatory remarks and

embarked on a discussion of the wonderful past of
Bel-rogas and the promise the future held. Sindi sat
back glumly and contented herself with surreptitiously
scrutinizing Yorgen peBor out of the corner of her eye.

So Kiv was going to marry her off, eh? His motivation in arranging such a match was perfectly transpar-
ent. Yorgen peBor was of the highest lineage, a direct
descendant of the great Lawgiver, Bel-rogas Yorgen.

Besides, Yorgen peBor's father was the Uncle of
Public Works, holding a pleasant and well-salaried
position, and his father's father was the oldest and most
respected member of the Council of Elders. Certainly a
marriage into that clan would be advantageous for Kiv
as well as for Sindi.

But yet—

She examined Yorgen peBor, sizing him up as a
prospective husband. He was big, not especially handsome in Sindi's eyes, though far from plain, and rather
stupid-looking in a genteel sort of way. He promised a
dull but pleasant kind of existence.

She thought of Rahn—penniless Rahn, whose father
was a pauper. Oh, well, she thought. We could never
have managed it anyway. Too many factors stood in the
way of their marriage.

And now, the biggest and bulkiest factor was Yorgen
peBor Yorgen. With a marriage all but arranged, Sindi
didn't dare tell her father she didn't like the idea.

She searched the crowd anxiously for Rahn, as
Grandfather Syg droned on and on.

I'd like to see him once more, she thought. *Just once.*

She glanced at her father, suppressed a little snort of
rage, and sat back to hear what Grandfather Syg had to
say. Yorgen peBor Yorgen appeared incredibly bored
with the whole thing.

The celebration was climaxed by a long ceremonial prayer. Sindi wanted desperately to close her eyes against the brilliance of the cloudy sky overhead, but she didn't dare to; her father would see. She didn't want to embarrass Kiv.

At last it ended. The assembly broke up, slowly, and Commemoration Day was over for another year. The multitude fragmented into little clumps of people.

Kiv turned to Sindi as the prayer ended.

"Now I can talk to you." He leaned forward. "Tell me—your letters were all so vague. Do you find the School as wonderful a thing as I did, Sindi?"

"Wonderful?" She looked puzzled for a moment. "Oh, of course, yes, Kiv." She had been enrolled for only three weeks. "I've been specializing in chemistry. It's very interesting. I have a little laboratory over in the back building, and I work there."

"A private laboratory?"

"No—not yet. They'll give me a private lab next year, if they like my work. No; I share it with another first year student. We work very well together."

Kiv stroked his golden fuzz reflectively. "That's good to hear. What's her name?"

Sindi paused. After a moment she blurted out: "It's not a her, Kiv. His name is Rahn peDorvis Brajjyd. He's a very good student."

"I see," Kiv said. Sindi could tell that he didn't care much for the idea at all. "Rahn peDorvis Brajjyd, eh? A relative, perhaps?"

"No. I asked him that, as soon as I found out we were of the same clan. His people are from up north, from Sugon. We're not related at all."

Kiv frowned. Sindi watched him anxiously, wondering what it was she had done wrong this time.

"Strictly speaking, you know," Kiv said, "that's not true. All Brajjyds are related, no matter how distantly."

"Oh, Kiv!" Sindi was annoyed. "Don't be so technical all the time. So what if his grandfather ten generations back was a cousin of mine? We're actually not relatives at all, so far as anyone cares."

"So far as the Law cares, you are," Kiv said. "Don't forget that."

At this point Yorgen peBor Yorgen cleared his throat in a meaningful fashion, and Kiv frowned apologetically. "But here we are, quarreling like hungry animals, and I've forgotten about poor Yorgen peBor. I'm sorry I was so impolite," Kiv said.

"You needn't apologize to *me*, sir," Yorgen said.

It was a good point, thought Sindi. In his overeagerness to be nice to Yorgen peBor, Kiv had committed something of a breach of etiquette by apologizing to him. No matter how grievously Kiv had offended the younger man, it was out of place for a Grandfather to apologize to anyone younger.

Kiv smiled inanely, trying to cover his blunder. He moved to one side to allow Yorgen to stand next to Sindi.

"Suppose I leave you two here," Kiv said. "There are some old friends I'd like to look up. Tell me—is the Earthman Jones still here?"

"He is," said Sindi. "But he's pretty hard to get to see. He's always busy and doesn't get around to the students very much any more."

"He'll see me," Kiv said confidently. "Don't worry about that." He walked away across the lawn, leaving Sindi to cope with Yorgen peBor Yorgen by herself.

"What's chemistry?" Yorgen asked her, as soon as they were alone. His broad, heavy face reflected an utter la⊂k of knowledge, and he seemed thoroughly complacent about the situation.

Sindi considered the prospect of spending the rest of her life in the well-meaning but clumsy embraces of Yorgen peBor Yorgen, and entertained some thoughts about her father and his political aspirations which were so vivid in their malevolence that she looked around fearfully to see if anyone had overheard.

II

Kiv followed the well-worn path to the main building, and entered the big Central Room where he and Narla had spent so much time, twenty years before.

It looked much the same as his memory told him it had been. The winding staircase leading to the students' rooms still stood massively in the center of the hall, a glossy monument of black wood. The old familiar benches, the rows of books along the walls, the arching windows through which the Great Light gleamed—they had not changed.

A boy came by, clutching a stack of books under one arm. Kiv looked at him, feeling a sharp twinge of nostalgia. The boy's body was bright gold and his eyes were wide and shining. He might have been the twenty-year-old Kiv come back to life.

Kiv stopped him.

"Can you tell me where I can find the Earthman Jones?" he asked.

"Jones' office is upstairs," the boy said. "But he doesn't like visitors."

"Many thanks. May the Great Light—"

But the boy must have been in a hurry. Before Kiv had completed his blessing, the boy had scooted away. Kiv shook his head sadly and climbed the well-worn stairs to Jones' office.

He paused before the door, then knocked twice, firmly. There was no reply from within.

He knocked again.

A soft, barely audible voice said, "Who's there?"

"May I come in?"

There was no answer. Kiv waited five seconds, then knocked again. After a short pause, the response came.

"Who are you, please?"

"Kiv peGanz Brajjyd," Kiv said loudly. Again, no response for a few seconds. Then the door clicked open, and the soft voice said, "Come on in."

Kiv pushed open the door and peered in. Jones was standing behind the chair next to the door. Kiv remembered the tired-looking, strangely alien blue eyes, the short, almost arrogant little beard, the smooth Earthman face.

"Well, it's been twenty years," Kiv said.

"Has it been that long?" asked Jones. "I've barely noticed. It seems like just the last week that you were here, and your wife—what was her name?"

"Narla."

"Narla. And you were doing research on insects— the hugl, as I recall, wasn't it?"

Nodding, Kiv stared at Jones.

"You're *old*," Kiv suddenly said. "I remember your beard—it was brown. Now it's silver—the way an Elder's body hair is."

Jones smiled. "The Great Light deals with all His subjects in one way," he said. "I have been on Nidor for sixty-one years, Kiv. One's beard does turn to silver in sixty-one years.''

He moved toward his desk, still littered as always with papers, and casually turned a sheet of paper face down, not concealing the action from Kiv.

''School records,'' he explained. ''It wouldn't do for the parent of one of our pupils to see them. Confidential, you know. That is your daughter, of course? Sindi geKiv? A tall, very slender girl? I don't know the students as well as I did in your day.''

''Sindi's my daughter,'' Kiv acknowledged.

''A fine girl. She'll make a better scientist than her father, they tell me—and we know how good her father was! We don't see many hugl any more, do we, Kiv? Thanks to you and your process, of course.''

''I'd almost forgotten about that. Almost. But I think of it every now and then. It was one of the high points of a life that's far behind me. But . . .'' his voice grew sad ''. . . though I'm a hero among the farmers, I'm afraid I'm not loved by the Edris powder manufacturers who I put out of business by wiping out the hugl. They had hard times on my account. Some of them still haven't regained a footing in society, after all these years.''

He shook his head. ''It's troubled me to think of the changes in Nidor since my days at Bel-rogas, Jones.''

The Earthman frowned. ''It troubles you? Why, Kiv? I thought you would be a happy man.''

''I'm a priest now. I'm no longer the young hothead I once was, when I confronted the Council. And I see the patterns changing, and it frightens me.''

''Have you talked like this to anyone else?'' Jones asked abruptly.

''No—no. I've only recently come to realize it. I've

been waiting for today, for this chance to discuss it with you. It's not only the Edris powder manufacturers. Other things are changing, too. The way children act, for instance. I'm thinking about my daughter.''

"Your daughter's merely a reflection of yourself, Kiv. Your thoughts, your opinions, all eventually are taken over by her. You've molded her. Perhaps the failure's yours, as a parent?''

Kiv studied his hands. Once again, Jones was the teacher, he was the blind, fumbling pupil. As it had been twenty years before, when Jones had led him, prodded him, pushed him into the knowledge that had enabled him to end the hugl menace, he was at Jones' feet.

"Is the failure mine? How could it be? I've lived by the Law and the Scripture—you taught me yourself. I've raised her with the greatest care. And yet—and yet—''

Jones stood up, chuckling. "*Your're* the one who should be retiring, Kiv. Not me.''

"What—retiring? Are you retiring?''

"Soon,'' said Jones casually. "The Great Light wants me, I fear. But you're the one who should go. You've turned into a terribly old man very quickly. You sit here, protesting about the behavior of the younger generation, even though you know it's foolish to protest. *Your* parents worried about the way you carried on, when you left the farm to come to Gelusar, and Sindi's probably going to think *her* children are deviating woefully from the Law. It's an inevitable pattern, bound up with growing old. But don't worry about it, Kiv. Sindi's a fine, Law-abiding youngster. She's a credit to you, Kiv. Don't ever think otherwise about her.''

Kiv stared uneasily at the old Earthman. "I see these

things, and yet you tell me—"

Jones rested his hands lightly on Kiv's shoulders. "Kiv peGanz, listen to me. The Edris manufacturers had to go. It was a natural evolution. You can't go around feeling guilty over it; what if you hadn't come up with your technique for killing hugl? We'd *all* have starved by now, not just the Edris makers. And your daughter's a good girl. Do you have any plans for her marriage yet?"

"I'm considering a high member of the Yorgen clan," Kiv said.

He felt less tense; after twenty years, Jones was still a master at the art of removing burdens from his students' shoulders.

Jones moved a thin hand through his silvery chin hair. "Have you made the formal arrangements yet?" he asked.

"Not quite. The Yorgens, after all, have a high position. It takes a great deal of negotiation. But the outlook is promising."

Jones looked out the window at the fading glow of the Great Light and nodded slowly. "It would require a great deal, of course." He said nothing for a long minute, still staring at the silver glow of the sky. After a while he said, "What does Sindi think of this marriage?"

Kiv frowned. "What does she think of it? Why, I don't know. I simply haven't asked her. Why? Does it matter?"

Turning from the window, Jones smiled. "No. Not in the least. Believe me when I say that this is probably the best decision you could have made."

"Then you do approve of my choice for Sindi's husband?"

Jones nodded. "I do. Most emphatically. I can't

think of a better choice you could have made.''

Kiv bowed his head. ''May your forefathers bless you, Jones. May they bless you.''

''Thank you, Kiv. And now, if you please, I would like to study. An old man must do many things in a short time,'' the Earthman said.

''You're actually retiring, then?'' Kiv asked. ''You weren't joking?''

''It's not something I'd joke about, Kiv. I feel that I've been called.''

''We'll miss you,'' Kiv said. ''And I think I'll miss you more than anyone else.''

''Thank you,'' the Earthman said again. ''And now—''

''Of course.''

Kiv bowed politely and left Jones' study.

When he returned to the courtyard, the crowd had already deserted it. Only Yorgen peBor stood there, leaning slouchingly against one of the trees, looking as though he couldn't care less that he was in the courtyard of the great Bel-rogas School. Kiv walked over to him.

''Yorgen peBor, where is Sindi?''

''I believe she has gone to her room, Grandfather,'' the young man said with an air of bored politeness.

He was wrong. That was the excuse Sindi had given him, but she had headed, instead, for the biochem lab, very much pleased to rid herself of the company of Yorgen peBor Yorgen if only for a few minutes.

And she would be able to see Rahn again.

Rahn peDorvis Brajjyd was a tall, hard-muscled young man whose fine down of body hair was just a shade darker than Sindi's. He was sitting at one of the lab benches, deeply absorbed in a frayed textbook, when Sindi slid the door open and entered.

"I thought I'd find you here," she said softly. "Didn't you see the ceremony at all?"

He grinned at her. "No. Not having a father who's a local dignitary, I didn't feel compelled to attend the affair. I stayed here."

Sindi half frowned. "That's not fair, Rahn. Besides, I wouldn't have gone either if Smith hadn't caught me in the stables. He made me go."

"Too bad," Rahn said, still grinning. "But I hope you won't get into any trouble because of it."

"I won't. Smith's all right."

She was silent for a moment, thinking out what she had to say next. "Rahn," she said finally, "do you know Yorgen peBor Yorgen?"

Rahn rubbed a hand over the soft down on his cheek. "I know *of* him, but I don't know him personally. Why?"

"What do you mean, you know *of* him?"

Rahn's shoulders lifted in a slight shrug. "He has money to burn. He's known to keep company with a girl named Lia gePrannt Yorgen, but don't go repeating that around. He's got the reputation of being a fast lad with a set of pyramid-dice and is known to take a drink or two occasionally. He has a sort of group of loyal followers from the—ah—poorer classes. They like his money. He's not too bright." Suddenly Rahn stopped and scowled at her. "Why all the interest in him? He's not coming to Bel-rogas, is he?"

Sindi shook her head. "No. I just wondered what he was like, that's all. He was at the Commemoration Day ceremony, and I was introduced to him."

She didn't feel like mentioning that it had been her father who had introduced her; Rahn would know at once what that meant, and she didn't want him to know—yet.

Again Rahn shrugged. "For all I know, he's a nice enough sort of fellow—just a little wild, that's all. I must say I envy him his money, though."

The girl put her hand on his. "Rahn, you're not going to bring that up again, are you?"

Shaking his head, Rahn put his free hand over hers, holding it tight. "Sindi, when will you get it through your head that I don't blame you or your father for what happened to my family's money?"

"But your father—"

"My father does, sure, but it was his own fault. If he hadn't been so stubborn, he'd have been all right. But he said that his father and his father's father and his grandfather's father had been Edris manufacturers, and his fathers before them for hundreds of years, and by the Great Light he was going to go on manufacturing Edris powder. He just couldn't understand what had happened when your father found a better way to use it, practically wiping out the hugl so there wasn't any need for tons and tons of the stuff any more. My father got hung by his own product. But just because Father can't accept change, just because he had to blame someone else for his own short-sightedness—that doesn't mean *I* feel that way."

"I know," Sindi said, squeezing his hand. "But I—"

There was a sound at the door, and she jerked her hand away from his. She turned around just as Kiv entered the lab.

"Hello, Father," she said sweetly, hoping she was managing successfully to cover up her alarm.

"I wondered where you were, Sindi." Kiv looked at Rahn and smiled politely. "How do you do, young man."

"I ask your blessing, Grandfather," Rahn said, bowing his head.

Kiv gave the blessing, and Sindi said: "Father, this is Rahn peDorvis Brajjyd, my lab mate."

"I am pleased to know you, my son." Kiv's smile hadn't faded a fraction. "PeDorvis? Isn't your father Dorvis peDel?"

"Yes, Grandfather." Rahn's voice was a little stiff.

"I think I met him, years ago. Take my blessing to your father when you see him next."

"I will, Grandfather," said Rahn politely. But Sindi knew he would never do it. The blessing of Kiv peGanz Brajjyd was something that Dorvis peDel would hardly care to accept.

"You must excuse us, Rahn peDorvis," Kiv said. "My daughter and I have some things we must discuss." He made a ritual gesture. "The peace of your Ancestors be with you always."

"And may the Great Light illumine your mind as He does the world, Grandfather," Rahn returned in proper fashion.

He stood silently as father and daughter left the room.

Outside, Sindi said nothing. She walked quietly next to Kiv, wondering what he was thinking. They had covered half the long paved roadway before Kiv broke his silence.

"He seems like a pleasant young man. At least he knows the greeting rituals and uses them. So many of the younger people today tend to forget their manners."

And that was all he had to say.

III

On the day of Jones' retirement, the students were asked to gather in the square. Word went round the rooms that a very special ceremony was to be held, and as the students filed into the square curiosity was evident on their faces.

Sindi and Rahn came straight from the laboratory, and got there late. They stood well to the rear of the clustered students, their backs pressed against the smooth granite wall of the Administration Building.

Unlike the recent Commemoration Day events, this was to be no public demonstration. Only the students and faculty of the School were present.

The rumors of Jones' retirement had been spreading for some time, and it became apparent that this was indeed to take place when the Head Grandfather of the School, fat old Gils peKlin Hebylla, made a short, dignified speech about how the Earthmen were emissaries of the Great Light Himself, and how the Great Light found it necessary to call them back when their work was done. The kindly old man was neither pompous nor maudlin about it; it was easy to see that he meant every word. Sindi fancied she could feel an undercurrent of personal emotion in his words, as though he were contemplating the fact that he, too, was approaching the Light.

When he was through, Jones rose slowly from his seat on the marble steps of the Administration Building. The Earthman looked at the hushed crowd for several seconds before he began to speak.

"Children," he said at last, "I have been here at Bel-rogas since the first—sixty-one long years. I have tried to show you, as best I could, what it means to follow the Law and the Scripture. I hope you have, by this time, seen where strict obedience of the Law may lead—or perhaps you have yet to see it.

"I have attempted to show you the wonders of nature that the Great Light has put here for you to see and use.

"I do not know how many of you will use this knowledge, nor how wisely you will use it, but you must always remember that the Great Light Himself will always answer all questions if they are properly asked of Him. The discovery of His way is the science of asking questions. And if you ask Him and he does not answer—then you have not asked the question properly.

"Ask again, in a different way, and you may have the answer. The answer lies in the question, not in the person who asks it.

"If the wrong person asks it, he may get the right answer, but he will not be able to understand it."

"I think I see what he means," said Rahn in an undertone. "Like in chemistry—if we want to know what a rock is made of, we have to analyze it. That's the right way to ask."

"*Shh!*" said Sindi sharply.

"Now the time has come for me to leave you," Jones went on. "I must return to the sky from whence I came. My place will be taken by a man who is quite capable of carrying on the great work that we came here to do. Smith has been with us for ten years, and has many years of work before he, too, is called back to his home.

"I wish you all well, children, and may the Great Light illumine your minds as He does the world."

As Jones held out his hand in blessing, Smith stood up and put his arm around the older man's shoulder for a moment.

"Goodbye, my friend," he said simply. "I'll see you again in fifty years."

Jones nodded, saying nothing. He allowed his arms to fall to his side, and he stood silently, straight and tall, somehow mysterious in his alien dignity.

Then, quite suddenly, an aura of blue-white radiance sprang from his body. Slowly, he rose from the steps and lifted into the air. With increasing speed, he rose higher and higher.

The crowd watched in awed silence, tilting their heads far back to watch the Earthman disappear into the haze of the eternal clouds.

Sindi was putting on her best shorts and beaded vest on the morning of the Feast of the Sixteen Clans, twenty days after the ascension of Jones, when her roommate burst into the room.

"Sindi! There's someone downstairs to see you! And is he handsome!"

Sindi fastened her belt at her waist. "Don't blither, Mera. Who is it?"

"Oh, you! Always so calm! I don't know who he is.

He just asked if Sindi geKiv Brajjyd was here, and so I told him you were. He's riding on a big, pretty deest, and he's tall, and—''

"Oh, Great Light!" Sindi swore in dismay. "I'll bet I know who it is! It's Yorgen peBor Yorgen!''

She ran out of the room and down the hall to the front of the building, where a window looked down over the courtyard before the Young Women's Quarters. Cautiously, she looked down, keeping herself well back in the shadows of the gloomy hallway.

It was Yorgen peBor, all right.

Come to think of it, Sindi thought, Mera was right. Yorgen *did* look quite striking, mounted on the magnificent deest and looking as if the whole world owed him homage.

I wonder what he wants? He would have to get permission to come calling here. And I'll bet he has it.

She ran back to her room and finished dressing quickly, ignoring Mera's bubbling conversation. Some minutes later she stepped out of the door of the dormitory, holding herself stiffly erect.

"Good Feast Day, Sindi geKiv," Yorgen said in his smooth tenor voice.

"Good Feast Day. What brings you here at this early hour, Yorgen peBor?"

"I started before the Great Light touched the sky," he said. "I have brought a letter from your father." He handed her the neatly folded and sealed paper.

Sindi thanked him, took the letter, and broke the seal.

"To my daughter, Sindi, on the day of the Feast of the Sixteen Clans. Since I know you'll be riding into the Holy City to attend the midday services at the Temple, I thought you would like someone to go with you. Young Yorgen peBor will deliver this letter and escort you to the Temple. I hope you will both find light in your mind and do your worship with reverence in your thoughts.''

It was signed, ''Your loving father, Kiv.''

Sindi looked up at Yorgen and forced a smile. ''I'll be most happy to attend the Clan Day services with you, Yorgen peBor,'' she said. In view of her father's note, there was no other possible answer.

''The honor is mine,'' Yorgen replied politely.

''If you'll wait here a few minutes, I'll get ready for the ride. My deest is in the stables, and—''

''May I get your animal for you?''

''Would you please? That's sweet of you.''

''Again, a pleasure, Sindi geKiv.'' Yorgen tugged at the reins, turned the deest smartly, and trotted off in the direction of the School's stable.

Sindi ran back into the dormitory, took the stairway at top speed, and dashed into her room. Mera was at the end of the hall. Evidently she had watched the whole procedure.

''What's up, Sindi?''

Sindi went to her desk and wrote furiously. ''I'm going to the Temple with Yorgen peBor,'' she said without glancing up.

''Oh? I thought you were going to the chapel with Rahn.''

''This is Father's idea, Mera. He has chosen Yorgen peBor for me.''

Mera frowned. ''I guess it's too bad you and Rahn are both Brajjyds. Still, in-clan marriages *have* taken place, you know.''

''Don't be ridiculous,'' Sindi snapped. She continued to fill the paper with neat script.

"Well," Mera said, "it might not be sanctioned, but I happen to know that a lot of young couples who are of the same clan just go to another city. The girl lies about her name and they're man and wife by the time they get there. You could go to Elvisen or Vashcor and—"

"Shut up, Mera. It's impossible. I couldn't leave Bel-rogas and neither could Rahn. I'll do things the way they should be done. I don't want to be sacrilegious."

Mera shrugged and said, "All right, do it your way. I still think it's a foolish law."

Sindi tightened her lips and said nothing. She finished what she was writing, folded it, and sealed it.

"Give this to Rahn, will you?" she asked, handing the letter to Mera.

"Sure, Sindi. Have a good time."

By the time Yorgen peBor Yorgen returned with her deest, Sindi was waiting demurely for him on the steps of the dormitory.

The five-mile ride into the Holy City of Gelusar was punctuated only by occasional small talk. It was obvious to Sindi that Yorgen peBor seemed no more anxious for the match than she was. But what could either of them do? Marriages were arranged by parents; their judgment was wiser in picking a mate than a child's could possibly be.

Gelusar was teeming with people in their holy day finery, each one walking or riding toward one of the several smaller temples in the city. Some of the more important people were going to the Great Temple in the center of Gelusar, but even that gigantic ediface could hold only a small portion of the city's population.

Naturally, as a grandson of the great Yorgen peYorgen Yorgen, young Yorgen peBor would have a reserved seat in the Temple itself. He and Sindi would not have to stand outside in the Square of Holy Light, as many thousands would have to do when the ceremonies began.

The square was, in fact, already crowded when they reached the Great Temple. They circled the Square and stabled their deests in the private stalls behind the huge building.

"If we go in the back way we can avoid the crowds," Yorgen peBor said. "There's a side hall that runs along the auditorium."

She followed him through the rear entrance. An acolyte stationed there to prevent unauthorized persons from entering nodded politely to Yorgen peBor and allowed them to pass. The hall was long and poorly lighted by the occasional candles that burned in sconces in the wall. Yorgen said nothing, not even holding her hand as they moved down the corridor.

Sindi wondered, for a moment, when her father would make the betrothal public. Actually, it was official now; only the ceremony was lacking.

The corridor came to an abrupt end, bringing up short against a massive door of bronzewood. Yorgen peBor twisted the lock and pushed it open. A low murmur of sound came through the opening, and Sindi could see the Temple auditorium beyond.

It was already beginning to fill with people. In the vast hush of the huge room, lit only by the gas mantles around the walls and the glowing spot at the altar, the golden glint of light against the bodies of the worshippers gave the temple an almost supernatural appearance. The people, to Sindi, seemed unreal—marionettes moving against a staged background.

It was the first time Sindi had ever been in the Great Temple on a feast day. Always before, she had gone to the Kivar Temple on the southern side of Gelusar. It was a small, almost cozy temple which made her feel as though the Great Light were actually there to protect her.

This was completely different. The huge lens in the roof of the gigantic auditorium was much bigger than any other glass lens on Nidor, and the light that came through it to strike the altar was brighter than any other spot in any temple.

What was it that the Earthman, Smith, had called the Great Light? A *blue-white star*. What did that mean? To Sindi, nothing. But it sounded mysterious and reverent, although without any concrete significance. And the light that streamed through the lens to be focused on the hard marble of the altar was neither blue nor white—it was a soft, golden yellow that seemed warm and friendly and powerful.

Yorgen was saying: "We'll have to move down toward the front, Sindi geKiv. Our pew is in the third row."

She followed him down the aisle with head bowed, as was proper in the Presence of the Great Light. When they reached the row of upholstered benches that was reserved for the use of the Yorgen Yorgens, Sindi slid in and kneeled before the glowing spot of light that rested just off the center of the altar. When it reached the exact center the ceremonies would begin.

"Uh—Sindi geKiv—I'd—ah—I'd like to have you meet a friend of mine." Yorgen peBor's voice, a conversational whisper, somehow sounded strained and hoarse.

Sindi turned her head to look. The girl was sitting on the other side of Yorgen and was smiling at her in an odd sort of way.

"Sindi geKiv Brajjyd, I should like to have you meet Lia gePrannt—Yorgen," he added almost reluctantly. "Lia gePrannt, this is Sindi geKiv."

Lia's smile broadened a moment, then relaxed. "I'm glad to meet you."

"As am I," Sindi returned. The girl was evidently one of Yorgen's relatives who—

Then she realized who. What was it Rahn had said?

He's known to keep company with a girl named Lia gePrannt Yorgen.

And then, quite suddenly, Sindi understood a great many things. She knew why the girl had given her such an odd smile; she knew the reason for Yorgen peBor's hesitation; she knew the reason why Yorgen peBor was so polite and formal toward her.

She found herself liking Yorgen peBor Yorgen.

She not only liked him, she *knew* him. She knew how his mind worked, and why he acted the way he did.

In that flash of illumination, Sindi geKiv Brajjyd learned a great many things. About others, about herself.

She looked at the glow of the Great Light upon the altar-top and smiled to herself.

Thank you, Great Light. You have illumined my mind.

Perhaps Yorgen was a blockhead; perhaps he was shallow. But in spite of the fact that she didn't love him, she at least knew him, and that would make their life together bearable. Perhaps, Sindi thought, the old ones were wisest after all. The old ways retained some merit. Kiv had not picked a worthless husband for her.

The glowing spot of light on the altar had reached the mirrored depression in the center.

It began to get brighter and brighter.

And then the great bronze gong that hung beside the altar was struck by an acolyte behind it. It shuddered out its ringing bass note, and the services for the Feast of the Sixteen Clans began.

IV

When they rode back to the Bel-rogas School, Yorgen peBor left Sindi at the gate. He thanked her for her company, assured her that he would like to see her again, soon, and rode back toward the city.

Sindi guided her deest toward the stables and dismounted at the door. She led the animal inside and took off the saddle. The stall next to hers, she noticed, was empty; Rahn had evidently gone into the city, then. Most of the students had attended the services at the School's small chapel, rather than ride into Gelusar.

She took a heavy, rough towel from its peg on the wall and began to wipe the perspiration off the back and angular sides of the deest. She was just through with one side when her roommate Mera came running into the stable barn.

"Sindi! One of the girls told me you'd just come in. Here! It's a letter from Rahn. He left it with me. He told me to give it to you as soon as you came back."

Mera held out the folded, slightly grimy sheet of paper. Sindi dropped the towel, snatched the letter from her roommate's hand, and tore it open.

''My dearest darling Sindi,

I knew this would happen—I suppose we both knew it. But I didn't think it would be so soon. You'll have to marry Yorgen, of course; you can never marry me. But I'm afraid to stay to watch it. I couldn't bear to see you betrothed to that deestbrained playboy.

I love you, Sindi, and I'll always love you. Try to think well of me. I wish you the best happiness.

Rahn pD.B.''

She stared at the letter, reading it a second time, then a third. She looked up at Mera.

"What is it?" Mera asked. "Bad News?"

"No—no," Sindi said, struggling to keep a calm appearance for her roommate's benefit. "Just a little note—about some lab work."

"Oh," Mera said in relief. "The way you looked when you read that had me worried."

"Don't be silly. And thanks for bringing the note down here," she said, as Mera started to leave.

Sindi folded the letter, tucking it in a pocket, and picked up the towel. The deest was heavily beaded with perspiration; for a few moments she let the work of wiping the animal off drive all other thoughts from her mind.

She went about her work methodically, finished caring for the animal, and headed back to her lab room. It was, she knew, the only place where she could really be alone, now.

Once she was inside, among the familiar, almost beloved pieces of apparatus, experiments-in-progress, dirty textbooks and heaps of soiled lab clothing, she bolted the door and sat down in a chair. Rahn's chair.

She read the letter once again.

I'm afraid I can't stay to watch it, it said. That explained why Rahn's deest had been missing from the stable. Rahn had run off somewhere.

Sindi thought of Rahn, quiet, serious-minded, a little shy, always polite and respectful, and then she thought of Yorgen peBor. Yorgen, who didn't love her, and Lia gePrannt, whom Yorgen did love.

And suddenly, with perfect clarity, the thought came to her that there was just one logical thing to do: go to Rahn, wherever he might be.

But where was he? Some cautious probing around the School made it evident that none of his few close friends knew where he might have gone to. Had he gone home? No; Sindi rejected the idea. Rahn's father, Dorvis peDel, was a proud and fierce man—even more so since his heavy fall. Rahn would never dare return home as a failure, to announce that he had left the Bel-rogas School for some trifling reason. Sindi tried to picture the scene that would result when Dorvis peDel discovered that it had been because of Kiv peGanz Brajjyd's daughter that his son had left.

No; it seemed impossible that Rahn had gone home.

The next strongest possibility was that he had gone down to Gelusar. If that were so, it wouldn't be an easy matter for Sindi to find him. Gelusar was Nidor's biggest city, and it would be simple for a lovesick boy to lose himself quite efficiently in it.

But the drawback there was that Gelusar was only five miles from the School, and there was fairly steady traffic between Bel-rogas and the Holy City. Gelusar was always full of people from the School; there was a fairly good chance that, in time, Rahn would be seen and recognized by someone.

Sindi rose and petulantly flipped on a burner, and

stared at the flickering flame until her eyes began to smart. Everything in the lab bore Rahn's imprint: the retort filled with some mysterious golden-green liquid standing just above their row of notebooks, the dent in the burner where Rahn had once dropped it, the untidy mementoes of his presence all over the lab.

There was one logical place where he would have gone, and as the answer occurred to Sindi it also struck her that she would have to get moving in a hurry in order to catch him in time. He would be heading for the seaport of Vashcor, Nidor's second largest city, three days' journey away on the other side of the forbidding Mountains of the Morning.

He had often talked of going to Vashcor. He had wanted to travel, to have adventure, and Vashcor was the gateway. Of course, Sindi thought—he had gone to Vashcor!

She drew a deep breath, tidied together some of the notebooks just to keep her tense hands busy, and took a few tentative paces around the lab while she decided exactly what she was going to do. Then she dashed out of the lab at top speed.

Her deest was waiting patiently at the hitching post, but the animal looked tired and not at all anxious to undergo a long journey. Glancing down at the other stalls, she selected the biggest and sturdiest animal there. It was Smith's.

Apologizing silently to the Earthman for the theft of his deest, Sindi unslipped the hitching rope and led the animal out of the stable. She leaped lightly into the saddle, which Smith had thoughtfully left in place, stowed her lunchpack in the saddlebag, and guided the deest down the winding turf road that led away from Bel-rogas.

Vashcor lay due east. The road was a good one, running up to the low-lying foothills of the Mountains of the Morning and then detouring around the great bleak mountains. No one ever went near the Mountains of the Morning. They were cold, nasty-looking peaks, bare of vegetation. The nightly rain of Nidor washed them clean of soil and left them standing, naked teeth jabbing up out of the plains.

Aside from their uninviting appearance, the Mountains were surrounded by an aura of taboo. They were dead and empty; for the Nidorians, anything dead was sacred, and hence somewhat to be feared.

But I'm going to go over those mountains, Sindi thought. *They won't scare me.*

It was a matter of necessity. Rahn had had several hours' head start on her, and unless she caught up with him he might easily reach Vashcor and ship out for points unknown before she could find him. If she detoured across the mountains, she might be able to make up the head start Rahn had, since he would go the long way, around them.

That is, she *might* be able to make up the difference. There was no guarantee the mountains were passable.

As she left the outskirts of the School and headed down the open road to Vashcor, she muttered a brief but heartfelt prayer. The Great Light seemed particularly bright that afternoon. She took it as a good omen.

The road traveled through perfectly flat countryside for mile upon mile. Far in the distance, half-hidden by the cloudy haze, she could see the Mountains of the Morning. Behind them was Vashcor.

The first part of the lonely journey took Sindi through fairly populous farm territory. The roads were hardly crowded, but occasionally farmers going to market passed her, recognized her School costume, and saluted respectfully. Occasionally, yokels called things after her as she sped by.

Then as the Great Light started to dim for the evening, the character of the countryside changed, and the farms became fewer and more widely spaced. Sindi became uneasy, and had some grave doubts about the wisdom of her wild venture, especially when it grew dark and the ever-present night-time drizzle of Nidor began.

Cold, hungry, a little frightened, and, before long, soaking wet through her light garments, she nevertheless urged the deest onward. Hour after hour passed; darkness closed in about her, only the faint glimmer of the Lesser Light breaking through the shroud of clouds. Her body became numb from the constant swaying and pounding of the deest. From time to time the animal needed rest, and it was then, when motion ceased, that Sindi realized fully how tired she was.

And then morning came, and she realized she had no idea where the night had gone. There was the sudden realization that the Great Light had returned gradually to the sky, and the rain had ended, and warmth was in the air, and that was all there was to tell her that there had been passage of time.

The Mountains of the Morning—the name seemed appropriate, now—were closer than ever before. They loomed up high on the horizon, huge purplish piles of stone. Certainly, Sindi thought, they were a grim and foreboding barrier for anyone contemplating a crossing.

The road was completely deserted now. Sindi kept staring ahead, hoping wildly to get some glimpse of Rahn, but there was no one in sight.

She continued relentlessly on through that morning, pausing once to give her deest an extended rest. The unfortunate animal was near the point of collapse. Sindi let the deest stretch out in the road for about ten minutes, and then, impatient to get on, prodded the animal up.

"Let's go," she said.

The animal broke into a weary canter, its doubly-cleft hooves clattering along the road.

After perhaps two hours of solitary riding, Sindi spotted a figure coming toward her in the road. For a moment she thought it might be Rahn—returning, maybe? but as the other drew near she realized it was an ancient man, riding a bedraggled-looking old deest.

She pulled up, anxious merely for the company of another person.

"Hoy, Father!"

"Hoy," the old man replied. He was dressed in rustic costume; probably he was a venerable farmer returning from a visit to Vashcor. "Where to, youngster?"

"Vashcor, Father."

"A long journey for one so young," the old man commented.

Sindi smiled. "I'll manage, Father. Tell me, old one: have you seen anyone else riding for Vashcor this morning?"

The old man thought for a moment. "Well, no. That is—by the Light, yes, I *did* see one. Young fellow, heading down the road as fast as could be."

Sindi said tensely, "What did he look like?"

The farmer chuckled. "Oh, I can't remember things like that, youngster. I don't see very clearly any more, any more. But he stopped to ask if he was on the right route to Vashcor. He wanted to know what the quickest route was."

Sindi rocked impatiently back and forth on her deest.

"And what did you tell him?"

"I said for him to keep going on the road he was on, of course. This is the best road to Vashcor." The old man paused again, and a frown added new wrinkles to those already on his brow. "But then I laughed and told him if he was really in a hurry he could make a shortcut over the Mountains, and blast it if he didn't take me seriously and say he'd do it! Last I saw of him, the fool was heading for the foothills. He must be crazy; no one ever goes near those moun—"

At that Sindi uttered a little gasp, dug her heels into the deest, and went charging away, leaving the old man still standing by the roadside. "May the Great Light bless you," she called back at him.

He had taken the mountain path? Sindi frowned, realizing that her planned shortcut was now no advantage at all in the race to head Rahn off, but a necessity. She stared up at the mountains, now quite close.

The road began to sheer off, going to one side of the mountain range, which was not a very wide one. As soon as Sindi became aware she had reached the detour-point, she cut off the main road and started across the gray-green fields at a sharp angle toward the Mountains of the Morning.

After a while the vegetation died out and bare desert appeared. And then Sindi spotted something that made her heart pound: well-defined deest tracks, leading toward the mountains.

They had been made recently. They could only be Rahn's.

She followed the trail carefully, and the land began to rise as she entered the foothills. The air was perfectly still. Not even a breeze broke the silent calmness, and no sound was heard.

It was hours later before the thin sand of the foothills could no longer hold the prints of the deest she was following. Here, so far as Sindi knew, no living person had ever gone. No one had ever had reason to; the Mountains of the Morning were barren, devoid of all life except lichen and small insectoidal creatures. Nothing that needed soil could live in these mountains; soil couldn't last long when it was floated away each night by the cooling drizzle that washed the planet when the Great Light was gone.

And now there was not even sand to register Rahn's tracks. Which way would he go? The easiest way, of course, Sindi answered herself. Whichever way that was, that would be the path she must take.

The path led over barren rock then angled higher and higher toward the summits of the peaks which loomed around her, giant crags, like broken teeth sticking out of a dead skull.

The deest was beginning to give out. His breath was short, and his strength seemed scarcely sufficient to hold up the weight of his own body, much less that of the girl on his back. Finally, Sindi dismounted and began to lead the tired animal. Her high-heeled riding boots were poor equipment for climbing across the bare boulders of the mountain, but she knew it would be even worse without them.

The daylight was beginning to fade again by the time she decided to sit and rest. How had Rahn gone on this far? She didn't know, but she knew that only a driving passion could push him on this far—an inverted passion, a passion that pushed him away from her instead of pulling him toward her.

She slumped down on a nearby crag of black basaltic rock and put her head in her arms, wishing gloomily that she had had the good sense to run off with Rahn

when the idea had first been suggested to her. If she
had, none of this would have—

Chunk!

Sindi jerked her head up and looked around her in the
fading light. What had made the noise?

The faint purr of a deest reached her ears. And then
she knew.

She climbed to the top of a nearby boulder and
looked around. There, only a few dozen yards away,
was another deest, grazing peacefully. But there was no
rider. The saddle had been removed.

Apparently Rahn, knowing he could go no further
with the animal, had relieved it of its burden and set it
free. And it could have taken place only a few minutes
before, Sindi reasoned—else the deest would have
made its way farther down the mountains, where there
was grass to eat and soft sod on which to lie.

Now, the deest seemed to be merely waiting for its
master to return. Rahn couldn't have left it very long
ago.

Sindi took everything she had and put it into the pack
on her back. Then, pulling the saddle off her deest, she
slapped the animal on the rump.

"Move off, fella. Go home. Smith is going to be
looking for you."

The deest trotted off. Sindi started up the rocky
incline, keeping her eyes open for places where Rahn
had disturbed the rockfalls, searching for his footprints
in the gravel.

Something had been driving Rahn, all right. He had
wanted so badly to escape, to run away to Vashcor, that
he had taken this insane route over the mountains.

The route that she, just as insanely, was following.

She kept moving, trying to ignore the pain in her feet
from the high heels of the riding boots she was wearing.

Upward, upward, as blisters formed on the soles of her feet. Upward.

And all the time she climbed, with each weary shove of foot against ground, she knew she was following Rahn into the place where neither of them really wanted to go—the one place where they could finally be free from the constricting network of age-old Nidorian customs and ways that bound them.

The one place where they could find peace together.

The Halls of Death.

V

The pale, colorless glow of the Lesser Light made the rocks seem like great lumps of bread dough as Sindi climbed. She moved higher, higher—

And suddenly, she realized she had heard a noise, had been hearing it for the past several minutes without paying any particular notice. She stopped climbing, to still the sound of her boots crunching against the gravel.

For a moment she could hear nothing; then the sound came again. A hum. A buzz. What was it? It was directly ahead, and it definitely was not the sound of someone climbing.

She listened for a few minutes more; reaching no answer, she resumed her climb.

Several minutes later she saw a flickering light not far ahead. Then, when she came over the edge of a little outcropping, she saw something that was so totally alien to her that it took a long time even partially to understand it.

It was a plain, a broad, flat plain. Acres and acres of ground had been levelled and smoothed and covered with concrete-like rock. And all around the edge were colored lights, some green, some red, some yellow, some white. Close to the edge nearest her were little buildings with lights on them and inside them.

What could this mean, she wondered. Who would build anything up here?

She stood for what seemed to her like a long time, trying to make sense out of what she saw. It was not until her eyes perceived something moving that she was jerked suddenly back to reality.

A squad of men was marching out of the darkness of the craggy rocks and heading through the lighted area toward the cluster of little buildings. Sindi frowned down at them for a second and then had to stifle a little scream.

They were Earthmen! That was unmistakable. And they were holding a Nidorian, forcing him to go with them to the buildings near the edge of the great field. Sindi knew who that Nidorian had to be; there was only one other in the Mountains of the Morning.

She acted almost without thinking.

As rapidly and as silently as she could, she ran toward the cluster of buildings to which the Earthmen were guiding Rahn. They had taken him inside by the time she got there.

She didn't know which room he was in; the entrance to the structure was on the other side, and she was unable to locate any door. All she could do was look for lighted windows.

There were several on the ground floor, but the rooms revealed were occupied entirely by Earthmen. Finally, Sindi found an outcropping of rock that would permit her to get close to the one lighted room on the second floor. The window was open, and the breeze of the chill evening air fluttered the papers on the desk in the room.

There were four men in the room—three Earthmen and Rahn. Sindi peered close—and then got a shock even greater than the last. For one of the Earthmen was Jones!

Jones—who had gone to the Great Light—was here!

He was saying, "I'm sorry you came here, Rahn peDorvis." Jones looked old and very tired. "It was never intended that any Nidorian should find this base." His jutting little beard waggled as he spoke, but his voice was as kindly as ever.

Rahn was staring curiously at the Earthman. When he spoke, his voice was tight and strange. "You're dead, Jones. Am I dead too?"

Jones shook his head slowly. "I am not dead, my son. I never said I was going to die. I said I was going back to the sky. And I am. But when I go, I will be alive. As alive as I am now. As alive as you are."

Sindi stared in amazement. It seemed to her that Jones was trying hard to convince Rahn that his words were true and honest.

Rahn's hands gripped the arm-rests of his chair. "But what does it all mean? I mean—well, that sounds silly, but—well—"

Jones held up one hand, palm outward. "I know how you feel, Rahn peDorvis. And I'll explain everything to you, believe me. You're capable of understanding most of it, and I think you deserve a full explanation. Do you want some water?"

Rahn had been licking his lips, but it was obviously fear and not thirst that motivated the action. Still, he did not appear to be overly afraid of the Earthmen. Sindi clenched her fists and prayed silently.

"Yes, Jones," Rahn said. "Please. Some water."

One of the other Earthmen poured a glass of water for him. Jones went on talking.

"I won't ask you how you came up here, nor why. That isn't important. What you want to know is why we are here and why we are doing whatever we're doing.

"The answer is very simple. We have come, as we told you, to help Nidor. Look—let me show you something."

He pressed a button on the desk near him. Behind him, a screen lit up. It depicted a scene in full color: a very odd-looking Earthman was dancing gracefully in miniature across the screen.

"Is that an Earthman?"

"Earthwoman," Jones corrected.

Yes, Sindi thought, gasping. It was an Earthwoman! Her head hair was long and golden and reached nearly to her waist. It swirled around her as she danced.

"This is an entertainment screen," Jones explained. "With this, we can see to any point within range. We can talk with each other and see each other."

He pressed another button. The Earthgirl in the screen vanished.

"As of now," Jones went on, "the average Nidorian must work very hard—many hours a day—to stay alive. We of Earth have machines that will relieve Nidor of this back-breaking work. We have machines that will cook food, plow the ground, build buildings, or solve complex mathematical formulas.

"We are trying to give these things to Nidor," Jones said. "The Great Light has brought us to you to guide you onward. *But it is not yet time*. You must become acclimated. You'll have to get used to the idea of leisure and a better life. You'll have to understand what it means to go to the stars before you can go there.''

"Stars?" Rahn asked.

"You'll find out about them too," the Earthman said. "We intend to help you reach space; to see the Great Light Himself, as we do—but we cannot help you there yet. The people of Nidor have too much to learn yet, and it is up to us to teach you.

"That's why we have to be careful. If you were given full knowledge now, your culture would come smashing down around your ears like a house of bricks built without mortar. And we don't want to wreck your culture that way. We want you to be happy with these things, not miserable with them."

Rahn nodded, though it was obvious to the watching Sindi that he did not completely understand. Jones signalled suddenly to the other three men in the room. As they grouped around Rahn, Jones said: "I'm afraid we can't let you remember these things, now that we've told you. We'll have to blank out a part of your memory. We'll have to remove all knowledge of this base."

"But—"

"Believe me, Rahn, it's the best thing for Nidor."

Rahn nodded resignedly. "If you say so, Jones. Will it hurt?"

Jones smiled, shaking his head. "Not at all. But tell me, now: how did you get up here?"

Rahn told how he had ridden his deest high into the mountains and then had gone on on foot. Sindi listened to him begin to explain *why* he had ridden out of Bel-rogas, but Jones cut it short.

"You call these mountains, but you haven't seen the really *big* mountains. The rain here, falling every night, keeps these mountains bare, and wears them low. Rahn, my son, you may not believe this, but I have seen mountains seven and eight miles high. The Mountains of the the Morning are less than half a mile at their highest peaks.''

Jones frowned then, and thought a moment. Finally he said: ''It's time now. We'll remove your memories of the past few hours. The machine is in the next room.''

Sindi watched as Rahn, obviously reluctant, rose and nervously followed Jones and the other Earthmen into the room adjoining. Sindi craned her neck to see into the room, failed, and edged around the building, looking for a window that would give her a clear view into the inner room. There was none.

What seemed like ages passed while she waited for some sign from within. Then, without warning, the door of the building slid open and the Earthmen appeared, bearing the unconscious body of Rahn.

Sindi shrank back against the wall, not wanting to be seen. She didn't know what it was the Earthmen had done to Rahn, but she was not at all in favor of having it done to herself as well.

To her amazement she saw the Earthmen rise into the air, carrying Rahn, and drifting down the cliff and out of sight—and there was no blue-white aura!

Sindi watched, astonished. All was silent, except for the constant hum and buzz of the base generators.

A few moments later the Earthmen reappeared, without Rahn. They floated gently up the side of the hill, entered their building, and vanished. The door closed behind them. Sindi edged out across the clearing and started the slow descent. As she lowered herself over the edge, she caught sight of Rahn, sitting at the base of the cliff. His deest was nuzzling nearby.

So they had removed his memories. And, effectively, they had silenced Sindi as well, whether they knew it or not. For who would back up her story? Not Rahn, certainly. Any tales she brought back would be discounted as mere wild imaginings.

But, more important, she had no desire to tell anyone of what she had overheard of the Earthmen's secret activities. What was it they had said—that Nidor was not yet ready? They were wise, and probably were right; Sindi did not want to say or do anything that might hurt the Earthmen's plans.

They held out the promise of a bright future. They beckoned to Nidor, keeping in reserve for them the wonders they had shown to Rahn. Someday, these things would belong to Nidor. If not to Sindi, then to her children. She would wait.

It was her duty to say nothing. The Earthmen were agents of the Great Light, and the Great Light would lead them to the promised land in his own good time.

In his own good time. It was promised. "Those beloved of the Great Light shall hold tomorrow in their hands." It was there, in the Eighteenth Section of the Scripture.

Rahn was dazed and bewildered when Sindi found him at the base of the mountain. He looked up in amazement as she appeared.

"What are you doing here?" he asked. Then he reconsidered. "On second thought—what am *I* doing here?"

"What happened, Rahn?" she asked quietly.

"I—I don't know. I left my deest here. I intended to climb on up—but—" He shook his head. "I don't know."

"Silly," she said smiling, "you fell. You hit your

head on a rock and it knocked the sense out of you.''

Rahn blinked, then grinned. ''I suppose—did you
see me?''

''No. But I've been following your tracks in the
gravel and sand for days.''

Rahn rubbed his head. ''My head hurts, and I feel
groggy. I'll never—'' He was looking toward the east,
and he saw the first glimmerings of the Great Light
rising above the horizon. ''The Light! How long have I
been—''

''You've been wandering around for hours,'' Sindi
improvised swiftly. ''I've found your deest. Mine got
away.''

Rahn put his hands to his temples. ''Let's go. Let's
go home. My—my head hurts.'' Sindi nodded silently.
Yes, she thought, *it hurts. I'll bet it hurts*.

Grandfather Kiv peGanz Brajjyd paced back and
forth in the outer office of Smith, the Earthman. Seated
on a heavy chair in one corner of the room was the
well-padded frame of old Grandfather Gils peKlin
Hebylla, his hands folded comfortably across his
paunch.

''Calm yourself, Grandfather Kiv,'' he said. ''The
children are on their way back. The telegraph message
from Gwilis Village said that they passed that way only
three hours ago.''

Kiv ceased pacing and clasped his hands anxiously
together. ''I know they're safe! I'm not worried about
that. But what about the betrothal? It's gone haywire
from both directions. What a scandal! What should I
do?''

The old man shrugged. ''Why worry? Young
Yorgen peBor has solved the problem for you. If he can

get a member of his own Clan — ah — in an — ah — interesting way and then talk old Yorgen pe Yorgen Yorgen into sanctioning their marriage, then you should have nothing to worry about.''

"Nothing to worry about?'' Kiv exploded. "Why, this is terrible! My daughter runs off with a member of her own Clan, and then the man she's going to be betrothed to finds that he is forced to marry a member of *his* Clan. Forced! Grandfather, do you realize that twenty years ago they would have been stoned to death? It's—it's *terrible!*''

"You're repeating yourself, my son,'' said Grandfather Gils quietly. "Remember, things change. Times are different today. Our society isn't what it was twenty years ago. We must remember that, you and I.''

Before Kiv could make reply, the door to the inner office opened, and Smith, the Earthman, said, "You wanted to talk to me, Grandfather Kiv?''

Kiv nodded. "Yes, Smith. If I might.''

"Come in.''

It was not Smith whom Kiv really wanted to see: it was old Jones he wanted, actually needed. But Jones had gone to the Great Light. Kiv would have to depend on the younger man.

He said, "I understand you'll have to expel my daughter from the School. I know that's proper, and I don't oppose it. But I want your advice on one matter. Should I permit her marriage to this Rahn peDorvis—a member of our own Clan?''

Kiv shuddered. All his plans now were destroyed; Yorgen was lost to him, and he was faced with the possibility, of an outrageous match between his daughter and the son of a penniless Edris-manufacturer.

Smith looked up from behind the massive desk and ran the tips of his fingers over his beard. "You're an alumnus of Bel-rogas, right?"

Kiv nodded.

Smith smiled quietly. "I fear you haven't taken your teachings to heart, then."

"What do you mean? I—"

"I don't mean to criticize your knowledge. But you've become too emotionally involved in this thing. Your thinking's clouded. Tell me: how do you interpret the Law as regards in-clan marriage?"

After a moment's thought Kiv said, "Well, there's nothing specific, but—"

"Actually. There is nothing specific. In-clan marriage is governed by custom. And what governs custom?"

"The practices of our Ancestors," said Kiv.

"Ah, yes. But who determines when customs should change?"

"Our Elders," Kiv replied. He felt as if this were some sort of elementary catechism.

"And who is Yorgen peYorgen Yorgen?"

Kiv shook his head stubbornly. "I can see what you're driving at, Smith. But it won't wash. Elder Grandfather Yorgen peYorgen permitted the marriage of young Yorgen peBor because he had been intimate with Lia gePrannt. It was the least unpleasant way of covering up an unpleasant situation. But no such thing has happened in the case of my daughter and Rahn peDorvis."

Smith folded his hands on the desk and closed his eyes. "Can you be sure?" he asked. "And if you can, can the rest of society be sure? It's not what you may think that matters—it's what society thinks. Is there, after all, any proof of Lia gePrannt's condition? Didn't the Elder Grandfather have to take that on faith?''

Smith jabbed a forefinger in Kiv's direction: ''There's your precedent, Kiv. Faith. It doesn't matter which way it may go; you have certain decisions you must make.

''Legally, your daughter can marry Rahn peDorvis, now that an Elder has sanctioned such marriages. Such marriages are now part of the accepted body of tradition. And isn't it your duty to your daughter to remove any stain from her name by announcing her betrothal?''

Suddenly, Kiv felt terribly small, and very confused. He fought with himself for a moment. He tried to picture how the Elder Grandfathers had felt, that day when a younger Kiv dynamically showed them how to wipe out the hugl threat. They must have been as confused and as puzzled, Kiv thought, as I am now.

Again a pattern was changing. And there was no help for it.

''I see,'' Kiv said quietly. ''I understand, and I accept what you've told me. I thank you for your advice.''

Smith nodded, smiling. ''I'm at your service any time, Kiv peGanz. And we'll be expecting your daughter and her husband back here at Bel-rogas as soon as they're through getting to know each other. They're the kind of people we want here.''

Kiv nodded, not daring to think any more. He gave the Earthman his blessing and walked out the door, uncertain of his attitude toward this new thing that had happened to Nidor, but still managing to keep his head high.

245th CYCLE

I

There were times in the following years when Kiv felt that perhaps Smith had erred in his judgment, but when he took time to analyze his thoughts, he realized that it was fatherly concern speaking, not any real fault in the young man who had married his daughter.

Rahn peDorvis studied hard, and often neglected his wife without realizing what he was doing, but he was never purposely unkind. Both he and Sindi were graduated with honors, and Rahn apprenticed himself to one of the Holy City's leading physicians, Syg peDel Lokness. The young man's knowledge of the strange teachings of the Earthmen puzzled Syg peDel on occasions, but the lad was a hard worker and had a fine capacity for learning, and was never disrespectful.

Once, when Kiv went to the old physician to ask how Rahn was doing, Syg peDel remarked: "He should do well, Grandfather. He's full of ideas, but he doesn't say much about anything until he's got it all worked out.

129

Sometimes, when I tell him something that I've learned through years of experience, he looks at me as though I'm repeating idle gossip—but he never says anything about it until he's checked it himself. And—I must admit it, Grandfather—a couple of times, he's taught me something I didn't know.''

Three years after their marriage, in the beginning of the Year of Tipell, the final year of the 244th Cycle, Rahn and Sindi presented Kiv with his new grandson. It was Kiv who suggested the name: Norvis peRahn Brajjyd.

From the very first, it was obvious that the boy combined the best qualities of both his parents. He had Sindi's good looks, determination, and quick wit, and he had Rahn's dogged persistence and depth of thought. Even as a child, he became absorbed in the work his father did, and by the stories his mother told. Once she even told him of the Earthmen's base in the Mountains of the Morning. She told it lightheartedly, hoping he would take it as it was offered, simply as a diverting story. But it made a vivid impression on him at the time; he took it as truth.

Rahn had a small practice of his own by the time Norvis could read, and the boy would sit around in his father's library, looking at the pictures in the anatomy books and struggling to fathom the meanings of the strange big words printed beneath them.

In the Year of Lokness, 245th Cycle, Norvis attended a ceremony that was to make a lasting impression on him. He was ten at the time, and understood little of what was taking place, but he watched avidly, silently, trying to comprehend all that he could.

The ceremony took place at the Great Temple of Gelusar, and every Brajjyd who could make it to the

Temple came to watch the investiture of the new Elder Grandfather of the Clan Brajjyd. The old Elder Brajjyd had become a Revered Ancestor only ten days before, having passed away in his sleep at the age of ninety-eight. The next in succession to the Council Elder of the Clan Brajjyd was Grandfather Kiv peGanz.

Norvis peRahn watched silently from a front seat while his mother's father took the Oath of the Council. After the Oath had been solemnized, the evening prayers were said, asking the Great Light to return on the next day to shed His blessings again on His people.

Norvis whispered to his mother, who was sitting next to him: "Mother, is Grandfather Kiv going to rule all of Nidor now?"

Sindi smiled. "Not quite, Norvis. He just *helps* to run it. No man could rule all of Nidor by himself."

Norvis thought the remark over and nodded. It made sense. He was to remember that simple sentence all the rest of his life.

There was no question of Norvis' future. Like his father and mother and mother's father and mother's mother before him, he would attend the Bel-rogas School. Like his father, his chief interests lay in the fields of biochemistry, medicine, and genetics, though his outside interests were wider than his father's ever had been.

He was a sturdy young lad, middling of stature but well built. He was an excellent swimmer and a top-notch deestman, and at sports he was neither a daredevil nor a coward. He was cautious. He had a tendency to calculate carefully before taking risks.

When he was younger, his bursts of temper were often astounding in their violence, but as he neared young manhood even his temper came under his policy of careful calculation. Only when outraged by absolute personal injustice did he have a tendency to strike blindly before he thought.

He was never very close to his mother's father, Kiv, but Grandmother Narla made a personal pet of the boy. The office of Rahn the Physician was a good mile from the house where lived the Elder Brajjyd, but, even as a boy young Norvis would walk the distance just to see his grandmother—and when he was given his first deest, he trotted proudly through the streets of Holy Gelusar to show it to his mother's mother.

When Narla's final illness confined her to bed, Norvis, now a strong, wiry boy of fifteen, went to see her every day. He wished his father were permitted to take care of her, for Rahn peDorvis was one of the finest physicians on Nidor, but custom forbade it. Old Syg peDel Lokness had been dead more than nine years, so it was necessary to call in another physician, Klin peFedrig Ghevin. Norvis had little liking for the man—but he was efficient enough, and knew his medicine.

When Grandmother Narla died, Norvis had difficulty accepting the fact. He sat, dry-eyed, all through the Passing Service, and then went out and walked up and down the streets, wondering why she had gone. He felt that the Great Light had been unjust in taking away his beloved grandmother—but how can one fight the Great Light Himself? Norvis' deep personal sense of justice was gravely offended, but there was nothing he could do.

The next day, he became entangled in a minor quarrel with one of the boys in the neighborhood. The boy was a year older and several pounds heavier, but Norvis suddenly struck out angrily and went at the boy with flailing fists. Within seconds, he found himself standing over an unmoving figure.

The boy was only dazed, not badly hurt. Norvis sat down and cried until the light down on his face was soaked with tears. And after that, he felt better about the loss of his grandmother.

He began at Bel-rogas in his seventeenth year, studying biochemistry and genetics as well as the Law and the Scriptures. He did much work directly with Smith, who guided him to deep understanding of his chosen subjects.

School was relatively uneventful until his senior year. That was the year that Norvis remembered ever afterward as the Year of the Ceremony of Lies.

NORVIS

I

The last thing that would have entered Norvis
peRahn's mind would have been a ceremony centering
around his esteemed classmate, Dran peNiblo Sesom.

Dran peNiblo being honored for something? Impossible, Norvis thought. Dran peNiblo was a bedraggled
little Nidorian from the slums of Tammulcor, and, as
far as Norvis knew, he had done nothing in his two
years at the Bel-rogas School of Divine Law but occupy
space in the classrooms.

Norvis shook his head, trying to clear the cobwebs
away. He had only had three hours of sleep; he had just
gone through a long, hard night of brooding and
work—mostly brooding, unfortunately—and he took it
most unkindly when young Krin peBor Yorgen, the
first-year boy who did the waking-up duties for Norvis'
floor of the dormitory, awakened him an hour before
the usual Bel-rogas reveille. Norvis was thoroughly
unhappy at the sight of Krin peBor's shining young face
peeking in the door an hour ahead of time.

"Rise and greet the Great Light, Norvis peRahn!" Krin exclaimed in an all-too-cheery voice.

Norvis opened one eye and squinted out the window. It was still gray outside; the Great Light was not yet bright in the sky.

"What in the Name of Darkness are you doing here at this hour?" Norvis asked irritatedly. "I've got an hour to sleep yet—maybe more."

"Not today," Krin said brightly. "Special ceremony this morning. Smith himself just came round to tell me to get everyone up early."

"Oh," said Norvis. He sank back under the covers, thinking that Smith had a lot of nerve calling a morning ceremony when he knew that Norvis had been up most of the night. He shut his eyes hard, trying to pretend it was all a dream.

A moment later, he opened them cautiously. Krin peBor was still standing there, arms folded.

"You'd better get up, Norvis peRahn," he said. "This is something special, according to Smith."

"He's not going to miss me," Norvis told him. "The School's big enough that they'll never notice I'm not there. Go away."

He slumped back and shut his eyes a second time, only to find Krin peBor shaking him vigorously by the shoulder.

"*Will* you go away?" Norvis asked peevishly. "I want to sleep—and you can tell that to Smith if you feel like it."

"Sorry," Krin said cheerfully, "But Smith gave me special instructions that you were to be there. So I guess you don't have any choice."

"I guess not," Norvis grumbled. Wearily, he dragged himself out of bed. "What's going on, anyway? You have any idea?"

"Sure," said Krin. "They're honoring Dran peNiblo. Giving him the Order of Merit, Smith said."

It took a moment to register. Then Norvis said: "*What?*" He sat down again on the bed. "Dran peNiblo? Being given the Order of Merit? For what? That fumblewit can't even find his way to class without having trouble."

Krin peBor shrugged. "I don't know why, either," he admitted. "But the Earthmen do funny things sometimes." He gave Norvis a look intended to convey deep meaning, but which merely seemed ridiculous on his youthful face.

Norvis shook his head. "Dran peNiblo! I don't get it."

It was, on the face of it, incredible, Norvis told himself as he reluctantly stood up again, still red-eyed from his long night of wasted effort.

"Well, at least that woke me up," he said, reaching for a fresh vest. "I couldn't get back to sleep without knowing what Dran peNiblo has done to deserve the Order of Merit."

Krin peBor, seeing that Norvis was definitely up to stay, smiled politely and ducked out. A moment later, Norvis heard him thundering on the next door down the hall.

Norvis stared balefully at the heap of papers on his desk, at the two or three scratched notes that had been the only products of his night's labors. His project was nearing completion—that was obvious—but last night he had come to the jarring discovery that, with the end in sight, he was not at all anxious to finish.

His specialty was biochemistry, and he had been working fairly closely on his project with Smith. Both he and the enigmatic bearded Earthman were sure that the project would probably make him a popular hero, a

member of the Order of Merit, and all the other things,
but some nagging doubt at the back of his mind had kept
him from handing in the completed work to Smith. The
worst part of it was that he didn't know *why*; he was
simply reluctant, and until he found the source of his
reluctance he was determined to go no further on the
project.

He scooped up the papers, shoveled them into his
file, and clicked closed the combination lock. Then,
smoothing his golden facial down with his palms to
make himself more presentable, he started downstairs.
From outside, he could hear the sounds of the gathering
which had started to form in the Square.

He still didn't believe it. Dran peNiblo being honored? For what? What was the little, two-legged hugl
capable of, Norvis wondered, that could ever make him
the center of any such affair?

For a bleary-eyed moment, Norvis considered the
possibility that it was all a hoax instituted by Krin peBor
for some obscure motive. It was unlikely, but it seemed
more conceivable than the idea that Dran peNiblo had
done something worthwhile.

Yet, when he emerged from the dorm and crossed the
Square to the main building of the School, he discovered that all was actually as Krin peBor had said. On the
little platform usually erected for such events, Norvis
could see the tall, solemn-faced figure of the Earthman
Smith, the rotund figure of Morn peDrogh Yorgen,
Head Grandfather of the Bel-rogas School, and, standing between them, looking impossibly thin and meek,
was Dran peNiblo Sesom.

It just doesn't figure, Norvis told himself as he drew
closer. *It just doesn't add up at all*.

He joined the outermost edge of the throng, edging in

to a little clump of upperclassmen who were standing together. They greeted him morosely; they were obviously almost as sleepy as he was.

"Did I hear right?" Norvis asked. "Are we all down here to see Dran peNiblo get glorified?"

"Precisely," said a tall, bored-looking student named Kresh peKresh Dmorno, who was from the western coast of the large landmass that was the larger of Nidor's two continents. "We are just discussing the utter improbability of it."

Norvis nodded and flicked a glance at the platform. Smith, Dran peNiblo, and Grandfather Morn peDrogh were standing there waiting for the School to assemble.

Smith, who had guided the School for years, who had been there in the days of Norvis peRahn's parents, was standing there, stroking and smoothing his graying beard, waiting calmly and patiently. Grandfather Morn peDrogh was darting nervous glances around, and occasionally turning to mutter something to Smith, at which the Earthman would hold up a hand in pardon.

Apparently the priest was apologizing for the tardiness of his students; Morn peDrogh was much more of a stickler for promptness and proper decorum than his predecessor, old Gils peKlin Hebylla, had been.

As for Dran peNiblo, the little fellow looked utterly ill at ease. As usual, his golden body hair seemed waterlogged and unkempt, and his eyes were dull and dreamy. It had long been a mystery to Norvis—and, apparently, to some of the others—how Dran peNiblo had managed to get past the Examiners. The Bel-rogas School of Divine Law was supposed to accept only the best, the cream of Nidorian youth. How did Dran peNiblo fit into that category? Some of the students had decided that Dran was unnaturally shy and afraid of people, and that made him seem stupid but the Earth-

men's tests had shown his true worth. But Norvis had
never subscribed to that rationalization.

Still, if he were going to get the Order of Merit,
didn't that prove something?

Norvis shook his head. He still couldn't buy the
theory. Dran peNiblo was fit to raise peych beans, like
any other peasant, or perhaps work in the stables,
tending deests. And yet, there he was, up on the platform, planted between Smith and the Head Grandfather.

Grandfather Morn peDrogh stepped forward and
raised both his arms above his head. The crowd stilled.
Norvis leaned forward to hear better. He was curious to
find out just what this was all about.

"My children," the Grandfather said in his solemn
voice, "Your attention, please." The priest waited for
the low hum of conversation to die out, smoothing his
hands against his blue tunic impatiently, then went on.

"We are here this morning to ask the blessings of the
Great Light upon one of our members. Let us pray."

Everyone turned to face the east, where the morning
glow of the Great Light was already showing a pearly
gray through the eternal cloud layer of Nidor.

"O Great and Shining Father," the priest intoned,
"Favor us this day by shedding Your Holy Light and
Your Ineffable Blessings upon us all. And favor especially those of us who have diligently worked in Your
Holy Cause. And favor especially one of our members
whom we, Your servants, are to honor today for his
work in Your Great Plan.

"Favor us, then, O Light of the World, by giving
special grace to Your servant, Dran, the son of Niblo,
of the noble Clan of Sesom, for the work he has done for
Your people."

The invocation was over. As one, the crowd turned back to look again at the platform.

Dran peNiblo still looked as snively as ever and as stupid as ever. Norvis felt it quite unlikely that the Great Light had paid any attention to the prayer.

Smith, the Earthman, stood up. "In order that all of you may understand what this young man has done," he said carefully, "we must take a look at the world's food supply and examine its fundamental nature.

"The principal crop, which is the basic plant food of all Nidor, is the peych bean," Smith said. "Now, while it is truly written, 'We do not live on peych alone,' it is, nevertheless, our most important crop. Because of its versatility, it may be used for many other things; its leaves provide us with fiber for our clothing; its stalks can be used as fuel or deest-fodder."

Norvis exchanged wry grins with the man standing next to him. "Next he'll be telling us that the stuff we breathe is air, and how important *that* is, he whispered.

"No," the other whispered back, "I think, after judicious consideration, that he will remind us that water is, after all, very wet."

From the platform, the Earthman's voice went on. "You can see, therefore, what a boon it would be if some method were to be discovered to aid the farmer in producing peych beans. Dran peNiblo has been concentrating on an approach to this problem.

"Those of you who have been studying agronomy know how the soil is enriched by fertilizers, of course. What Dran peNiblo has done, very briefly, is discover a way to increase the per-acre yield by nearly one hundred percent, by means of a new growth hormone which—"

Norvis peRahn's wandering attention snapped back

suddenly to what the Earthman was saying. Growth hormone? It couldn't be! That was his own pet project!

He strained his ears to hear Smith's words more plainly.

"—which permits the plant to make more efficient use of the soil. Although the cost of producing this new substance is high, very little is needed for each plant—a matter of a few drops sprayed over the leaves of the plant itself.

"Naturally, the exact process will remain a secret, to be kept in the possession of Dran peNiblo and his descendants in order that he may reap the proper profit due him by virtue of his brilliant work."

Norvis peRahn felt the golden fuzz on the back of his neck prickle. *Smith had quoted almost exactly the words in his own notebook, locked upstairs in his file!* He sputtered in rage. Why, that little sneak of a Dran peNiblo had stolen his work!

Norvis rocked back and forth for a second or two, much too bewildered to be able to say or do anything at all. The events of the entire morning had been insane, unbelievable.

On the platform, Smith, with a great show of ceremony, had taken a small box from his voluminous robes and had handed it to Grandfather Morn peDrogh. The Grandfather turned to Dran peNiblo, who had yet to open his mouth. He was standing there, smiling insipidly.

Grandfather Morn opened the box and brought forth a magnificently embroidered ribbon with a gleaming bronze medallion dangling from it. The assembled students suddenly became terribly quiet.

"Dran peNiblo," said the priest sonorously, "kneel."

The little man knelt humbly. Grandfather Morn

looked upward, where the Great Light gleamed through the ever-present clouds, and then down at the kneeling Dran peNiblo. Norvis froze.

Solemnly, the Grandfather said: "The Blessings of the Great Light be upon you, Dran peNiblo, for the brilliant work you have performed here at the Bel-rogas School. It is only fitting, then," he continued, starting to slip the ribbon around Dran peNiblo's thin neck, "that we, by virtue of the power vested in us by the Council of Elders, do hereby invest you with full and unqualified membership in the Gracious Order of—"

Norvis could take no more.

"*Stop!*" he roared.

The sound of his voice broke the dead silence that had prevailed in honor of the investment. Norvis heard the single word ricocheting off the buildings and echoing back, bouncing around the Square.

All eyes turned on him. He felt terribly alone in the midst of the crowd.

"What does this interruption mean?" Grandfather Morn asked sternly. His eyes were blazing with rage.

Norvis took a step backward, only vaguely noticing that everyone around him was edging slowly away, leaving him standing, a solitary figure, in the midst of a cleared circle. He tried to speak, but he could find no words.

"I repeat," the Grandfather said. "What did that outburst mean? By what right does a student irreverently interrupt a Ceremony of Investiture?"

Again Norvis struggled to speak, and this time the words were there.

"Dran peNiblo is a *thief!*" he shouted. "The growth hormone was *my* project! He stole it from me!"

Some of Grandfather Morn's rage seemed to be replaced by shock and wonderment. "That is a very

serious and unusual charge," he said cautiously.
"What proof can you offer?"

Norvis pointed a golden-haired finger at the tall
Earthman. "Ask Smith, Grandfather! Smith knows!
He knows I was working on it! I'm almost finished with
it! Go ahead, Smith!" Norvis stopped suddenly. The
Earthman was saying nothing, but there was a look of
detached surprise on his alien face.

"Well?" said Norvis hoarsely. "Go on, Smith! Tell
him! Tell them all that Dran peNiblo stole my project!"

Norvis felt his hands quivering. He was no longer
afraid, not even of the Earthman; he was burning with
righteous indignation. *"Go on!"* he shouted. *"Tell him
all about it!"*

Smith looked almost sorrowfully pained. "Dran
peNiblo has been working on this project for over a
year," he said quietly. "He has been reporting to me
regularly. I know of no other project in the School
which is even remotely similar."

Grandfather Morn peDrogh frowned. Obviously, the
whole scene was very distasteful to him, and he was
unsure of how he was going to recapture the dignified
tone of the ceremony.

"You have heard the Earthman?" he asked sternly.

"It's a lie!" Norvis yelled. *"I* was working on the
project! Dran peNiblo wouldn't know a hormone from
a deest's bray without a picture-book! That was *my*
project, and he stole it—and Smith *knows* that! Smith's
lying! *Lying!"*

Overcome by rage, Norvis pushed his way through
the crowd, heading blindly for the platform, where
Smith awaited him, arms folded calmly.

Norvis kept repeating, over and over again, "Smith
is lying! The Earthman is lying!"

Then, quite suddenly, a powerful hand was clamped

over his mouth, and two more seized his arms. He
struggled, kicked wildly, bit at the hand. It had the alien
odor of an Earthman's skin, and then Norvis sensed the
acrid taste of an Earthman's blood. But the hand remained where it was.

He was in the grip of two of the Earthmen, and they
were dragging him away, back from the platform, then
further away and into one of the buildings. He continued to fight and struggle, and, as he was hurled, still
protesting, through an open door, he heard the droning
voice of Grandfather Morn peDrogh proceeding with
the ceremony as if nothing had happened.

II

The long road that led from Holy Gelusar, the capital, to the great eastern seaport of Vashcor veered to the southeast to avoid the Mountains of the Morning, a branch of the mighty range of the Ancestral Mountains that ran east-and-west across the continent, separating the rugged northern province of Sugon from the more fertile plains of the south.

The traffic was not heavy along the road; the easiest method was to take the river packet from Gelusar, traveling down the Tammul River to the southern seaport of Tammulcor, and then take a coastal ship around to Vashcor. But that cost money, and Norvis peRahn had precious little of that. He had six twenty-weight notes in the wallet of his vest, and two six-piece coins in his pocket, making a hundred and twenty-one weights in all. Not much money to last a man very long.

He tried not to think of his personal problems, but with every loping step of the long-legged deest beneath him, they kept pushing their way back into his mind. A glance at the bleak crests of the Mountains of the Morning reminded him of the story his mother had told him long ago—about a secret place of magic that the

Earthmen had hidden somewhere in those jagged peaks. Sindi iRahn had told the story many times, always cautioning young Norvis not to tell anyone else, and at the same time instilling in him a certain uneasiness about the Earthmen—a suspicion that had been more than amply confirmed now.

The sight of the mountains, reminding him of his mother, reminded him in turn of her tears when she learned that he had been expelled from the Bel-rogas School as a result of the scene he had caused that day.

The first student expelled in the four-generation history of the school had received a lukewarm reception at home. His father had tried to understand, but it was obvious that he did not believe Norvis peRahn's story. After all, would an Earthman lie? And where were the notebooks that Norvis claimed to have kept? Why weren't they in his locker?

Norvis had tried to explain that they had been stolen—taken by the Earthmen while he was out of his room, watching the ceremony. But his explanation had fallen on deaf ears.

Grandfather Kiv peGanz had been positively icy, but just. The gruff old man had given him money for the trip, and asked him to take himself as far from Gelusar as he could get. There were no jobs open for young men who had publicly disgraced themselves, their family, and their Clan by calling an Earthman a liar and trying to take credit away from a deserving fellow student.

And so, alone and more than a little bewildered, Norvis had left Gelusar, all his proud hopes ended.

The road to Vashcor was not a short one to begin with, but even the easy loping gait of the deest he was riding could not soothe the anger that boiled up inside him, and that anger only seemed to make the journey longer.

Why had the Earthmen lied? Why had the notebook been stolen? And why, above all, had the secret been given to that runted little blockhead, Dran peNiblo Sesom? Obviously, Dran had thought that the hormone process *had* been invented by himself. Smith had, therefore, been giving the little hugl information from Norvis' notes for nearly a year, and making the fumblebrained Dran think it was his own work. But why? Was it because his great uncle was Grandfather Golis peGolis Sesom, one of the most powerful of the Elders? But what difference would that make?

None of it made any sense. The only thing that made sense was his deep hatred for the Earthman, Smith. And the other Earthmen, too. McKay and the others must have known what Smith was doing. They must have known that Norvis peRahn would denounce the theft—otherwise, why would two strong Earthmen have been standing in readiness, prepared to drag him away from the ceremony as soon as he had opened up?

For some reason known only to themselves, the Earthmen had contrived to ruin his life. They had stolen the secret that would have made him famous, and they had stigmatized him in the eyes of the world forever. Why? What went on in the alien brains behind those strange eyes?

Norvis peRahn turned the problem over and over in his mind during the long journey, but he never seemed to come up with an answer.

The Grand Harbor of Vashcor shimmered greenly in the diffuse illumination of the Great Light. Here and there, like queerly geometrical trees, were the tall masts of seagoing vessels, and dotted among the bigger ships were swarms of smaller boats rolling lazily on the incoming tide.

Norvis peRahn watched one ship as her sails caught the
wind at the harbor mouth and she moved majestically
out into the open sea. The Grand Harbor was almost
ideally sheltered, surrounded as it was by high cliffs
which protected the bay from the wind. The little
paddle-wheeled steam tugs pulled the bigger ships out
to the harbor mouth, past the cliffs, to where the wind
could push them out to sea. Then they would wait until
other ships came into the channel and tug them into port
when their sails dropped and sagged idly in the still air
of the harbor.

It was almost unbearably hot, even for Norvis, who
was used to this sort of weather. The humidity made his
body hair cling to his skin; he felt sticky and uncomfortable. He also felt hungry.

He wasn't quite sure whether he should eat immediately or wait until he got even hungrier. He was
beginning to wish he hadn't been in such a hurry to sell
his deest. After eighteen days, his money was getting
low, and he hadn't found a decent job yet. Oh, there
were plenty of jobs around, if a man was willing to do
just any sort of thing. Street cleaning, stable sweeping,
bilge washing, hull-scraping work at the drydocks—
none of them appealed to Norvis, and none of them
offered any chance of advancement. Still, if things got
much worse, he might have to take on a menial job just
to eat and pay the rent on the small hole-in-the-wall
room he had found.

The trouble was, all the decent jobs were pretty well
sewed up by the guilds. Of course, the letter he had
from Elder Grandfather Kiv peGanz Brajjyd *might*
allow him to get past the guild barrier—but he thought
not. It would have, ordinarily, but the news of his
expulsion had already preceded him to Vashcor. No
one would want anything to do with him when they
found out who he was.

There was one other way. It was rough work, but if a man had brains, he could get somewhere eventually. Norvis watched the flying sea-lizards floating lazily in the faint updrafts and thought the proposition over.

Finally, he took a three-piece coin from his shorts pocket and flipped it into the air. The bronze disc twinkled as it spun up and dropped back into his hand.

If it came down "prayers," he'd try job-hunting for another five days; if it came down "price," he'd go to the Shipmaster's.

He grabbed it out of the air and slapped it down on the back of his arm. He looked down, wondering if he'd see the lettering of the prayer inscription or his graven figure 3.

The number looked up at him from below the triangular hole in the center of the coin. It was "price."

The Shipmaster's was a huge, square building that had been erected a thousand years before. The stone, like that of any other ancient building, was weathered and pitted, and the stairs that led up to the main entrance were deeply worn by the passing of hundreds of thousands of shod feet.

The man behind the desk marked *Mercantile Enlistments* was wrinkled and old; his facial down was silvery with age.

"Good day, Ancient One," Norvis said politely. "May the Great Light bless you."

"Bless you, too, son," said the oldster sharply. "What do you want?"

"Enlistment in the Mercantile, Ancient. Any openings?"

The old man narrowed his eyes. "There's always openings for a man who likes the sea. What's your name?"

"Norvis peKrin Dmorno," Norvis lied. The Dmorno Clan was large and mostly concentrated in the far west; it was a safe alias.

"Can you read and write?"

"A little," Norvis admitted cautiously. He didn't want to admit that he had had much schooling, but it might be difficult to completely conceal the fact that he was literate.

"I have an opening for a scrubhand, usual four-year terms. Do you know what that means?"

"Stay on four years. Money is paid at the end of the enlistment. If I skip ship, I forfeit all rights to the money."

"That's it," said the old man. He pushed a piece of paper and pen across the desk. "Sign the bottom line."

Norvis glanced over the paper and then looked up. "This is an eight-year contract. I only want four, Ancient One."

The old man pulled the paper back. "You *can* read, I see. All right, try this one." He pushed out another paper. This time, Norvis signed.

It was an old trick; if a man couldn't read, they'd hand him the longer term contract. He would think that he was free after four years and come to the office to collect his pay; often he'd miss his ship. Then—no money.

Norvis knew that his first ship would be going to the Bronze Islands for metal cargoes. They wouldn't take a chance on giving a new man a ride around the coast; he simply might be trying to get back home again for nothing. They couldn't let him skip ship at his home port after only one voyage.

The old man gave him a slip of paper. "Go back to Room Thirty-four. You'll be assigned to the *Balthar*, under Captain Del peFenn Vyless."

Norvis nodded and headed for Room Thirty-four.

Four years of life at sea helped Norvis become sure of himself. He started out cleaning ship and waiting on the crew. The sailors, all guild members, did nothing but sail the vessel; none of the dirty, grimy jobs for them. That was for the swabhands, not for skilled labor.

It wasn't an easy life, not for a man used to the comparative luxury of the School. He took orders, but he didn't take them happily at first. But he was careful always to carry them out to the best of his ability; it wouldn't be wise to get jugged out of his sole remaining source of income.

After the first two trips, he found himself starting to rise aboard ship. He grew in responsibility, and the sailors began to accord him the privilege of a greeting. It was obvious to all, particularly to Captain Del peFenn Vyless, that this was an unusual swabhand; he quickly rose to first rank among the swabbers—a small victory, true enough, but a victory, nonetheless.

At the end of his first year aboard the *Balthar*, Norvis was eligible for membership in the guild, and he was voted in by overwhelming acclaim of the full-fledged sailors on board, with Captain Del's hearty approval. They gave him his certificate on the first really long journey they undertook, out around the coast to the distant seaport of Sundacor. Someone had painstakingly inscribed "Norvis peKrin Dmorno" on it, and he smiled over it; for all intents and purposes, Norvis peRahn Brajjyd was now dead and forgotten. It was just as well.

He rose rapidly in the guild; at the end of his second year, he was elected Spokesman by his fellow crew members, in deference to his eloquence and superior intelligence. By now, there was more than a little speculation aboard ship on the topic of Norvis peKrin's doings before joining the Mercantile, but he said nothing, and no one asked.

From there, the step up to the hierarchy was rapid and inevitable. He was made second mate by Captain Del peFenn—a powerful, dynamic man with an overbearing bass voice and a vivid contempt for some of the most deeply-rooted Nidorian mores. Captain Del came from a long line of ship-owners, and the seamen of Vashcor had always been fairly detached from the theocratic mainland life.

For long hours, as the *Balthar*, wind in its billowing sails, moved in dignified fashion over the sea, Norvis would sit, watching, quietly nodding, while the Captain would express opinions which would undoubtedly have resulted in his stoning, were he a landsman. Gradually, the Captain unburdened himself more and more bluntly. He feared the power of the Council of Elders, who had immediate control over his cargoes and were always happy to tithe him at both ends. He bitterly resented this, as had his father before him and *his* father, no doubt, but it was the first time Del had had a chance to unload this resentment to another.

Norvis, without committing himself, managed to let the Captain see that he was at least in partial agreement. It took an effort occasionally, for Norvis did not actually hold the same animosity toward the Council that the Captain did, and when Del peFenn spent the better part of one evening attacking the Elder Grandfather Kiv peGanz Brajjyd, it was all Norvis could do to restrain himself. After all, honor and love for one's ancestors was set forth on the very first page of the Scriptures, and, as little as Norvis cared for old Kiv, he still respected him, both as an Elder, and as his mother's father.

Del peFenn's grievance against Kiv was a simple one; his father, Fenn peFulda Vyless, had held a stranglehold on the shipping of Edris powder from one part of the world to another. When the youthful Kiv's revolutionary hugl-killing methods had ended the entire Edris industry, old Fenn peFulda's contracts had been voided, leaving him temporarily bankrupt.

Even though his fortune had been rebuilt, and his son Del had increased it twofold, he had retained this bitterness until he died, and his son had carried it on. Captain Del peFenn returned to the subject of Kiv peGanz Brajjyd more than once.

As the months moved on, the Captain and his former swabhand grew quite close. And when, in the third year of Norvis' first enlistment, a prematurely lowered boom carried Charnok peDran Yorgen, the *Balthar's* first mate, overboard, never to be recovered, who else would be the logical replacement but Norvis peKrin Dmorno?

As first mate, Norvis moved up to the second-best cabin, just next to the Captain's, and his wage went up considerably. In odd moments, it pleased him to contemplate the amount of money that was accumulating for him, to be paid in a lump at the end of the four-year voyage.

Each time the ship put into port, it was his task to supervise the loading and unloading of cargo, and to break in the new men Del peFenn was forever hiring. The swabhands had the occasional habit for jumping contract, apparently preferring to lose their pay for a year rather than sweat out three more of the same, and hardly a stop went by without some new swabhand coming aboard. They were generally tall, gawky boys, too restless to make good farmers, and not clever enough to get into Bel-rogas.

After a while, Norvis came to realize why his rise to the top had been so easy; he was a veritable intellectual giant among sailors. Since every sailor began as a swabhand, and since the swabhands were always green boys, without education or any particular ability, a man with several years of the Bel-rogas School behind him stood out aboard ship like the Great Light over the mountains.

And then, on a warm afternoon in Norvis' final year of duty, Ganz peKresh Danoy joined the crew.

"We've got a new swabhand," Captain Del told Norvis. "He's down on the forward deck now, getting some of the smell of the sea into his lungs."

"Another green kid, eh?" Norvis said. "Well, I'll try to make a sailor out of him."

The Captain smiled. "You'd better go down forward and see him before you make any decisions." There was a strange light in the Captain's eyes, and when Norvis got his first look at Ganz peKresh Danoy, he understood.

Ganz peKresh was no green recruit—not by thirty years or so. He was a man of middle age, short, stooped, and not very intelligent looking. His blunt, flat face had the blank and bewildered appearance of a man whose life had been shattered after fifty years of complacent routine.

"You're the new swabhand, boy?" Norvis asked, just barely managing to conceal his disbelief.

"That's right, Ancient," said he, "Ganz peKresh Danoy, Ancient." He spoke in a dull monotone, and his voice had the nasal twang of a farmer from the bleak, hilly province of Sugon.

"You're older than our usual run of men, you know."

"I know. But this is all I'm fitted for." He spread his hands in an eloquent gesture of defeat and despair. Norvis felt a sudden twinge of premonitory fear.

"What do you mean?" he asked.

"Sir, you don't know? What's happened to us, I mean?"

Norvis' expression became grim. "No," he said slowly. "Suppose you come back to my cabin and tell me all about it. I'm somewhat out of touch with things." It was not the custom for officers to invite swabhands to their cabins, but Norvis wanted to be sure this was a private conversation—and his respect for custom was rapidly dwindling, anyway.

III

The story Ganz peKresh unfolded was a gloomy one. He had been, as Norvis had guessed, a farmer from Sugon. He had had a small tract of barely marginal land in the southern tip of the province, in the foothills of the Ancestral Mountains. The farming there had never been profitable in the first place; the hundreds of small farms there, raising peych-beans almost exclusively, operated on just the flimsiest dividing line between profit and loss—with loss meaning starvation.

Norvis knew the situation in that part of Sugon; he had studied it, back in those almost forgotten days when he had been working on the growth hormone project. He suddenly grimaced at the memory. He had succeeded in burying it deep, the whole sordid business of the trumped-up ceremony for Dran peNiblo, his own expulsion and discrediting, and everything else. And now it came flooding back and hit him hard.

"Something the matter, sir?"

"No—no," Norvis said. "Suppose you get on with your story. How come you left your farm?"

"Well," Ganz peKresh said hesitantly, "it—it was this new thing. The new thing the Elders have. I don't know what it is, but all of a sudden I couldn't sell my crop."

Norvis stiffened. Those *Earthmen!* he thought savagely. All the old hate and bitterness surged up again now. He set his jaw. "Tell me." he said, trying to seem sympathetic. "Tell me all about it."

"There's not much to tell. The Elders got something from that School to make their farms prosper, and suddenly the price of my beans dropped to nothing. I—I—I had to sell my farm. I couldn't meet the competition."

"Coming from the School, eh? And they gave it to the Elders?"

"That's right, Ancient. There was a big ceremony at Gelusar, I remember. I heard that people came from all over. And one of those Earthmen presented whatever this was to the Council and—and the next I knew, Elder Danoy bought my farm from me. The only way I could support my family was to go to sea. So here I am." He smiled with a false gaiety; it was a weak, pathetic attempt at expressing an emotion he did not feel.

Norvis stood up. "The Elders kept it themselves, eh? Just like them," he muttered. *They took my hormone,* he thought, *and of course produced it in a limited supply—all of which the Elders took for themselves.* He paced up and down, ignoring Ganz peKresh. *So the Elders are getting richer, and the small farmers are being squeezed off their land.*

He turned. "All right, Ganz peKresh. That'll be all for now. I'll explain your duties in the morning."

Norvis sat alone in his cabin for a while after the ex-farmer had gone, struggling to control himself. He felt, once again, the same righteous indignation he had experienced on that long-gone day in the square in front of the main Bel-rogas building, when he had shaken his fist at an impassive Smith and called him a liar in front of the whole School.

What did the Earthmen want? Why were they doing this? It could only be the Earthmen. They were the ones who had stolen his notes, who had trumped up his expulsion, who had seen to it that the Council of Elders had managed to get control of the growth hormone. Naturally, with the already rich Elders growing wealthier, and with the greater supply of peych-beans bringing down the asking price and cutting the small man out of the bidding, the Earthmen's actions were going to have disastrous consequences for Nidor's carefully balanced economy, which had been happily stable for thousands of years. There was no room in it for a small, tight group of very wealthy men, and a large group of itinerant, landless ex-farmers. And that was exactly the situation that was being created.

Deliberately! The Earthmen were deliberately changing the old ways, twisting, distorting, burying the Scripture and the Law under the weight of their innovations and manipulations. Norvis shivered with the strength of his realization; it occurred to him that he might be the first Nidorian ever to suspect that the Earthmen were not as virtuous as they claimed to be. It was a staggering thought.

"But it's not too late to return to the old ways," Norvis said aloud. The Earthmen had been on Nidor not ninety years, and ninety years was but a moment in Nidorian history. Surely the vast weight of four thousand years of tradition could overcome less than six cycles of meddling. The damage could be undone—if someone acted in time.

Norvis blew out the candle and went on deck to find the Captain. Del peFenn liked to stand this watch himself; it was a long-ingrained custom of his.

"Hoy, Captain!"

"Hoy, Norvis." The Captain was standing alone on deck, with the evening drizzle beginning to dampen him. He was staring out into the grayness; the Lesser Light was out, and its faint beam illuminated the harbor of Gycor.

"I've just been talking to the new man, Captain."

"Oh?" Del peFenn did not look around, but continued to stare out at the shore lights of the sleeping city. "Did you find out what a man his age is doing signing up as a swabhand?"

"Yes," Norvis said. Quickly, he explained how Ganz peKresh had lost his farm, not bothering to mention his own part in the development of the growth hormone.

Captain Del cursed vividly when he heard the whole story. "Those Elders! It's a wonder the people don't fight them! How many thousands of years is it that we've lived so infernally at peace?"

"The Elders aren't at fault, sir. It's the Earthmen who are responsible," Norvis asserted.

"Hmmm. Maybe so," the Captain said, after some thought. "But I've never trusted those old men anyway. They're probably conniving with the Earthmen right down the line."

"Sir—"

"What is it, Norvis?"

"We're heading for Tammulcor next."

"That's right. Straight around the coast to Tammulcor. Why?"

Norvis nodded. "I'm going to ask for my release when we get there. I think I could do something about this whole business—at least I'm going to try."

"You're crazy," Del told him calmly. "You can't fight the Elders. The whole world's bound to them hand and foot. It's always been that way."

"I'm not thinking of fighting the Elders, sir. I don't want to fight anyone. I just want to open people's eyes! They're all blind, every one, and they're being led right over a cliff!"

Captain Del was silent for a long while, and there was no sound aboard the ship but the steady splatter of the rain against the wooden hull of the ship, and the plinking of the drops into the water of the harbor. After a while, he said: "You'd be smarter to stay with me. My son is just a baby, Norvis; I need help now. If you stay with me, you might just find yourself a ship-owner yourself, some day." He turned from the rail and faced the younger man. "I've been thinking of buying another ship. I'll need a good man to be her skipper."

Norvis shook his head slowly. "No, sir," he said. "I appreciate all you've done for me—but I think I've got a job on the mainland."

"Very well," the Captain said. "I won't hold you back. I'll give you your release at Tammulcor. But I want you to know I'm not anxious to lose you."

"Thank you, sir."

"And when you come creeping back here with your tail tucked between your legs, remember that there'll be a place for you aboard this ship any time."

"You don't seem very confident that I'll get any-where, do you, sir?"

"No," said the Captain. "No, I'm not."

The rain continued to pour down. Neither of them said anything further.

Norvis went ashore at the huge port of Tammulcor, four years' pay weighing down the pockets of his seaman's tunic. The first thing he decided to do was spend some of it on clothes; a sailor's uniform would be somewhat conspicuous in inland Gelusar, and he had no intention of calling attention to himself until he had made a few inquiries.

He bought several well-tailored vests and shorts, and packed them into a new clothing carrier. Then he checked on the schedule of the next river packet upstream to the Holy City. He found he had a few hours to kill.

So, still wearing his uniform—common in a coast town like Tammulcor—he strolled into a waterfront beerhouse and ordered a glass of the heavy, warm brew that was the favorite drink of Dimay Province.

"The Great Light illumine you, barman," he said. "What's the news from Holy Gelusar?"

"May he illumine us all," replied the barkeep. "I've heard nothing much, seaman. Just about the same as yesterday." It was the common reply, and meant nothing. If there was any news, it was yet to come. "That will be one piece and two," he went on, setting down the tankard of foaming brew.

"One and two?" Norvis repeated in surprise. "That's rather cheap isn't it?"

The barman nodded as he took the money. "It is. A tankard has sold for one and six as long as I can remember. My father, great be his name, sold it for that, and so did his revered fathers before him. It covered expenses well. But now, with the peych-bean selling so cheaply, making the brew is cheaper, too. Others cut their price, so I had to as well. But it doesn't matter; the profit's the same, and that's all that matters."

Then he paused and looked toward the north. "News from Gelusar? There is some, I think. There have been more farmers who have lost their holdings all over Nidor, of course, but most of them have been around the Holy City. However, it's been said that the Elder Grandfather Kiv peGanz Brajjyd is still holding out. He won't use the new fertilizer-stuff on his own farms; he says it's not according to Scripture.'' The barman grinned. '' 'Course, he hasn't said anything about it in the Council. I dare say he ain't intending to get the other elders riled.''

"I've been at sea for four years," Norvis said. "How come only the Elders get the whatever-it-is?"

"Oh, it's not *just* the Elders. There are others who are getting some of it, but not many. Seems as though the stuff was invented by one of the Elder Grandfathers' nephew, or some such. Anyway, it took a lot of money to build the equipment to make it, so this Elder got some of the others together, and they chipped in to back the boy. The understanding was that they could get first crack at it, and what money they made would be used to make a bigger plant so the other farmers could get the stuff, too. It's a long-range plan, of course, but it's a good one. After all, I understand there was difficulty three hundred years ago, when they brought the steam engine in. It'll take time, that's all. Just time."

"I suppose so," Norvis agreed. *So Grandfather Kiv peGanz is still holding out, eh? Interesting.*

He finished his beer and laid coins on the bar. "Here you are, barman. That's the extra four you should have made."

"May the Great Light illumine you, sir." He scooped the coins off the bar with a practiced hand as Norvis strode out of the bar.

Norvis spent the rest of the time before the riverboat left walking the streets of Tammulcor, thinking over what he'd learned. So little snot Dran peNiblo was in business now, eh? Making himself quite a pile, too, no doubt. And by stealing another man's work!

Well, we'll see about that, me buck! The Earthman, Smith, was pulling a fast one on all of Nidor. Of that, Norvis was sure. The setup was obvious. What they intended to gain, he didn't quite know—but then, who could ever figure out how an Earthman thought?

According to them, they had all come from Heaven, the abode of the Great Light, but Norvis wondered if they might not have come from the Outer Darkness— the Edge, far out across the Eternal Sea, where the sky met the water. Weren't there demons out there, according to Scripture?

Demons or not, whatever and whoever they were, they were trying to ruin the old, tried-and-true ways of Nidor. By giving the growth hormone to the Elders, they were running the little farmer out of business and making the Elders richer. It was all right for a man to make money, and a monopoly was all right, too, but not when it threatened the lives of thousands of little men.

Something would have to be done.

When the riverboat arrived in Gelusar, Norvis peRahn no longer looked like a sailor. He was just another well-dressed middle-class citizen. After he found a small room in a hotel, he took a walk toward the capital's produce district, where the great peych-bean warehouses were. There, he could find out more about the situation.

It didn't take him long to find out; he could hear the hubbub all up and down lower Temple Street.

Farmers with deest-carts loaded with threshed peych-beans were blocking the street, straining, sweating and swearing. He could see how it would be on Chilz Street, where the cut stalks were taken, or in

Yorgen Square, where the long, fibrous leaves were pulped and made into cloth.

Pushing his way through the throng, he headed toward the Trading Building. There was a great deal of milling about, but Norvis' attention was caught by a large group of men who were listening to a red-faced peasant talk in an emphatic voice.

"I tell you," said the peasant, "something's got to be done! We'll have to petition our Elders—*all* of us! We're being ruined! I'm sure the Elders will change their minds when they see what's happening here!"

A chorus of "Yeas" went up approvingly.

"It would be different if things were getting better," he went on. "But they're not! They're worse! Two years ago, when I brought my crop in, they said the warehouses were full—*full!* And for thousands of years, our warehouses have only been seven-tenths full! They refused to buy, except at a lower rate! 'A quick sale,' they told me, 'so we can unload the warehouse.'

"But they haven't unloaded! This new thing the Elders are using makes the beans ripen earlier, so they sell their crop first! It just isn't fair, I tell you!"

"What should we do, Gwyl peRob?" shouted one of the crowd.

"Petition! That's what! We must all get together! They'll understand!" He nodded his head vigorously.

"All right," said another, "we'll petition and ask them to reconsider their plans. I'm a Sesom! Who'll go with me to speak to the Elder of our Clan?" Several of the crowd moved off with him, and another man stood up and declared his Clan as well.

Finally, Norvis stood up. "I'm no farmer," he said loudly, "But I'm a Brajjyd! And I say the Clan must stand together! I'll go with you!"

"Who are you?" It was the red-faced speaker, Gwyl peRob.

"My mother's father is Elder Grandfather Kiv peGanz Brajjyd," Norvis said evasively.

"Good, Clansman!" said Gwyl peRob Brajjyd, "You'll be our spokesman, then! Come, we'll round up others, too!"

It took two days for the committee to get an audience with the Elder Grandfather. None of the farmers paid any attention to the name "Norvis peRahn" when its owner finally admitted to it, and he decided that all the scandal about his dismissal from the School had either not penetrated to the farming class, or else had simply been forgotten.

But he knew Grandfather Kiv peGanz had not forgotten. When the two days, which Norvis had used for private investigations of his own at Dran peNiblo's factory, were up, and the acolyte took Norvis and his little delegation into Kiv's study, the look on Kiv's face had none of the friendliness one might expect from one's mother's father. Norvis met Kiv's cold glare for a moment, and seeing that four years had not altered the old man's sternness, he knelt in the ritual bow.

"The peace of your Ancestors be with you always," Kiv said. His voice had no warmth in it.

"And may the Great Light illumine your mind as He does the world. Ancient Grandfather," said Norvis. He stood up. "How is my mother, Grandfather Kiv?" He wished, suddenly, that he had gone to see her; perhaps—

"What do you want?" asked Kiv bluntly, ignoring the question.

Just as bluntly, Norvis replied: "I want to talk to you about this hormone business. I want you to talk to your fellow Council members. You've got to show them what this new hormone is doing to Nidor.''

Kiv smiled delicately. ''My fellow Council members are well aware of what they are doing, Norvis peRahn.'' He paused. Norvis saw that the old man was waiting for the ritual apology; but that was the last thing he would do. The Scripture, Norvis decided, would have to be put aside for the sake of getting something done.

He waited just long enough to make Kiv uneasy and the rest of his delegation thoroughly uncomfortable, and just when everyone was beginning to fidget, he said: ''These people are Brajjyds.'' He indicated Gwyl peRob and the other farmers with him.

Kiv nodded. ''I assumed they were Clansmen,'' he said.

''They're *starving*,'' said Norvis loudly. ''The new hormone, and the almost exclusive use of it by the Elders—don't you see what it's doing to them? They can't sell their crops! The warehouses are full!''

''I know,'' said Kiv in a quiet voice. ''My own farms do not make use of the new hormone, and my overseers are reporting difficulties along the lines you mention.''

''How does the stuff square with Scripture?'' Norvis demanded.

''I— don't know,'' said Kiv. He stared past Norvis, focusing his eyes on the symbolic lens of the Great Light in the niche in the wall above Norvis' head. ''That is why I have not used the hormone myself.''

''But the Council—''

''The Council as a group has approved use of the hormone, on the recommendation of Smith.'' He spread his hands. ''I am a minority.''

''Can't you fight?'' Norvis asked.

''I have yielded to their greater numbers,'' said Kiv.

"They are willing to trust the word of the Earthman, and I do not wish to quarrel. I prefer not to use the hormone myself, but I cannot publicly take a stand against the will of the Council as a whole."

Norvis looked from one member of his delegation to another. They were standing in a tight clump, and it seemed they were more awed by the immediate presence of the Grandfather than they were concerned with their own pressing problems. Norvis told himself that they had not been through the same embittering experiences he had, and thus they were still able to cling to the old faith.

He looked back at Kiv. "You won't help us, then?"

Kiv smiled. "You haven't made it clear just what help you require, Norvis peRahn."

"Certainly I have," Norvis retorted hotly. His words reverberated loudly in the little chamber, reminding him of that day when they had echoed through the Square at Bel-rogas. "I want you to go before the Council and demand abolition of the hormone!"

He felt Gwyl nudge him gently with an elbow. "Norvis—you're speaking to an elder," he said in a frightened whisper.

"Let me handle this," Norvis muttered. "Well?" he asked aloud.

"I have told you." Kiv spread his hands. "I have yielded to the Will of the Council." He closed his eyes, as if he would brook no more debate.

"But it's ruining Nidor!" Norvis shouted. He was angry now; the obstinate old man was deliberately refusing to see beyond the end of his nose. "Forty years ago, you nearly ruined everything with your Edris adaptation, and now you're letting the same sort of thing happen—only we won't recover so quickly!"

The Edris reference evidently stung Kiv. He

straightened in his seat, and what had been the remainder of his earlier smile sharpened into a grim frown. "I can do nothing. The Council has decided. This audience is at an end."

"You can't throw me out like this!" Norvis sputtered. "Why won't you think? Why won't you look at—"

"*This audience is at an end,*" Kiv peGanz said icily.

Norvis started to say something, but he felt the pressure of Gwyl peRob's hand on his arm, and subsided. Drawing a deep breath, he said: "All right. If you won't do anything, *I* will. I'll take the matter into my own hands."

"Please go," Kiv said. Suddenly he seemed very old and tired. "This audience is at its end."

Norvis, still raging, barely managed to control himself. "I'll go," he said. "But remember—the Council has had its chance. From now on, this is in *my* hands!"

He turned and stalked out, pushing the door open himself, without waiting for an acolyte to do it for him. The delegation of Brajjyd farmers followed him.

When they were outside, Gwyl peRob confronted him.

"Norvis peRahn, you failed us. That was a *most* irreverent way to address a Council Elder! Particularly your own mother's father."

"Failed you? I haven't yet started! You heard what I told him! From now on, this is in my hands. I'll talk to Elder Grandfathers the way they ought to be talked to!"

"I don't like it," the farmer said stoutly. "It seems to border on blasphemy. Why should you talk in such a way?"

Norvis realized then that at least a part of his anger at his grandfather had been caused, not by the old man's present attitude, but his attitude of four years before.

But he brushed the thought aside; there was other work to be done.

"Gwyl peRob, I think you'll find that our failure was not my fault. I'll be willing to bet that none of the other delegations have had any more luck with their Clan Elders than we Brajjyds have. We've got to do something big—something forceful, that will make the Council sit up and look at the problem of our people— all the people, not just Brajjyds or farmers, but all Nidorians. I want you and the others to help me get the people together so that I can talk to them. Will you help?"

Gwyl peRob turned it over in his mind for a moment. Then:

"I will help, yes. The people of the Clans have a right to know what you are planning. But they might not like what you say."

"Don't worry; I'm not advocating any violence; all I want to do is show them how to act peacefully, within the Law, to get justice. Now, come on; we've got work to do."

IV

The mass meeting had been called for late evening. Every farmer in town had been asked to show up at Shining Lake Park for a special address by Norvis peRahn Brajjyd, whose mother's father was the Elder Grandfather of the Brajjyd Clan.

Word had spread throughout the city that something was to be done about the worsening of the peych-bean situation, and by the time the Great Light had gone to rest, a sizable crowd had gathered in the park. Torches had been set up in the holders that ringed the Speakers' Platform.

It was something new to the people: a speech given without a formal occasion. Normally, the platform at the lake's edge was used for scheduled rituals or for concerts held by the various musical groups in Gelusar who wanted to perform for the public.

At the appointed time, Norvis stood up on the platform and raised his hands to silence the murmuring of the crowd. They were used to being addressed by a priest or a public official, so they quieted down immediately, despite the fact that Norvis peRahn was, properly speaking, nobody.

"In case you don't know who I am," Norvis began, "I'm Norvis peRahn Brajjyd. You all know what our trouble is: this new thing the Earthmen have given out. This new-fangled hormone that doubles the crops of the Elders and robs those who don't have it of their proper share of the crop money."

He paused and surveyed the crowd. It was growing larger by the minute, and it was a restless, shifting group of people. All the better, Norvis thought; it meant they were unhappy with the state of things.

"Farmers are being ruined!" he roared. "Men who have held their land all their lives—whose families have held it for a hundred generations, since the times of our many-times-great-grandfathers—these men are losing their land! They are being forced to leave that sacred ground!"

As the crowd began muttering, Norvis smiled inwardly; he was beginning to reach them.

"We know what is wrong, and we know that something has to be done about it. The question is: what are we to do?

"We have petitioned our Elders, and we have been put off. Our requests have been denied. And do you know why? I'll tell you why! We've been going about it the wrong way! We've been asking for help and not getting it because we haven't been attacking the problem in the right way."

He raised his voice to continue, "What does the Scripture tell us? 'To destroy a thing, cut at the root and not at the branch!' And what is the root of this evil? Where has this spawn of Darkness, this demoniacal growth hormone come from? What is the source of this substance which has been ruining our lives and is beginning to ruin our very culture?''

Norvis waited a moment and then shouted: "From where? *From the Earthmen!* It is they—not the Elders—who must be approached! The Elders do the bidding of the Earthmen! When an Earthman says *jump!*—they jump!''

The crowd was growing angrier and angrier by the moment. Norvis saw black frowns, heard mutters of wrath. He noticed, then, that Gwyl peRob was moving through the crowd, whispering something to people, stopping at a small knot of people, talking, and then moving on to the next.

Norvis grinned inwardly. The little, red-faced farmer was probably telling them how he had been treated by the Elder Brajjyd.

Norvis watched their anger grow. He saw that it was his moment to spur them even further.

"They are trying to ruin our lives! You all know how things have changed in Nidor since they came; our old system is breaking down! A hundred years ago, no Elder would have ignored a proper petition from his Clan. I say we must destroy this evil! And we can only do that by destroying the Earthmen! Their Bel-rogas School is a sacrilege against the Name of our Ancestors!

"The Earthmen—"

He got no further. A clod of dirt struck his chest, and he was astonished to hear someone shout: *"Blasphemy!"*

"Do you know who this Norvis peRahn is?" yelled someone else. "He's the blasphemer who was expelled from the School four years ago!''

"That's true!" shouted another voice. Norvis turned

his head to look. It was Gwyl peRob! "I found it out
only an hour ago! It's the same man! Twice he has
smeared the Light-given Name of Brajjyd!"

Another man roared: "I'm a Ghevin! Slandering a
name is one thing—but to slander the Great Light is
blasphemy!"

Norvis blinked. "But I didn't say—"

"Stone him!" cried someone. "False prophet!"

"Blasphemer!" cried another.

Norvis was paralyzed. He hadn't realized—

He snapped out of his shock when a rock thudded
against his ribs, almost knocking the breath out of him.

Amid shouts of "Sacrilege!" and "Blasphemy!"
and "Kill him!" Norvis peRahn Brajjyd turned to run.
Another rock struck his back. The crowd, spurred on by
a few of its more vociferous members, was beginning to
get murderous.

"He preaches against the Great Light!"

"Stone him!"

Norvis leaped off the back edge of the platform,
clearing the balustrade that ran along its rear edge.
Twelve feet below him was the water of Shining Lake.
As he hit the water, stones splashed all around him,
thrown by some who had swarmed up on the stage to get
at him.

"Get the torches!"

"Bring lights!"

"Find the blasphemer!"

"Someone call a peaceman! Call a priest!"

Norvis ducked underwater and swam as though his
life depended on it—which it did. There was only one
way to go; directly across the lake. It was long and
narrow, and he could make it across before anyone
would be able to get around it. And he was fairly sure no
one would try to swim after him.

They didn't, but there were a few pleasure boats tied up at the shore, and some of the pursuers got into them, carrying torches raised over their heads to illuminate the water.

Norvis came up for breath and saw that he was far enough away from the boats to chance swimming on the surface.

"Where is he?" someone shouted.

"I think a rock hit him!"

"Yes! I hit him with a rock just before he went down!"

Someone was trying to make himself a reputation, Norvis thought.

"Maybe he's drowned!"

"Let's keep looking! We've got to make sure!"

Norvis swam rapidly and quietly for the opposite bank, hoping he'd come out of the lake alive.

When he reached the Grand Harbor of Vashcor a good many days later, after a torturous and unpleasant hitch-hike with a foul-breathed deest-peddler who had been heading that way, he made his way almost immediately to the small, squat little hotel down in the fishermen's quarter of the city. He was in a dismal mood.

He registered under the peKrin Dmorno alias and was shown to a dingy room overlooking the sea. His room was unpainted and smelled of fish, but it represented the first sanctuary for Norvis since his flight from Gelusar. He had barely managed to get out in one piece, and he was glad of a place where he could sit down and rest.

The outlook was gloomy. He had botched things on all sides; Bel-rogas had long ago been lost to him, and his abortive crusade to prohibit the use of the growth hormone had only resulted in his alienation from *both* sides; the people had stoned him as a blasphemer, and were now perfectly content to let the Elders squeeze them dry in the name of Scripture.

It was a bitter ending; now, he realized, he had accidentally pushed the Elders into a stronger position than they had been in before. The populace was always ready to do something irrational if they could find theological grounds to do it on, and he had given them grounds with his blasphemous talk. They still held firmly to the old beliefs, and they'd keep on doing so, even if it ruined them—which it was doing.

He frowned and walked to the window. There was a cluster of ships in the harbor, and he squinted out, trying to search out the familiar masts of the *Balthar*. He didn't see it, but his way seemed clear; he would abandon the pack of them. Nidor and its Elders could go their merry way to Eternal Darkness; Norvis would throw his lot with Del peFenn or some other free sea-captain and hope that things didn't get too bad during his own lifetime. It was an unheroic way out, but he was a miserable failure as a hero.

The next day, he made inquiries. No, the *Balthar* was not in port, he was told. Yes, it was due back soon from the Bronze Islands, and have you heard about the blasphemer who was killed in Gelusar?

Norvis got that bit of news from one of the men at the Shipmaster's Building. He pretended he had heard nothing, and was told the whole tale, with most affecting and grisly particulars.

"A grandson of the Elder Brajjyd, eh?" he said, shaking his head. "What's that Clan coming to?"

"It's a disgrace, an utter disgrace," his informant agreed.

Norvis nodded. "But they killed him?"

"Of course! Bashed his skull in with a rock! Blood all over the water. He never came up again."

"Well, then, we needn't worry," Norvis said, "His ideas stand no chance of being spread, then."

"A blessing indeed," agreed the other.

Norvis was overjoyed at the report of his death. The excitement of the mob, the exaggerations of witnesses, the boasting of a couple of rock-throwers, and the red gleam of torchlight on the water had added up to death. It meant that no one had seen him slip out of the far side of Shining Lake and make his way out of Holy Gelusar. He was free, now, to bury Norvis peRahn Brajjyd forever and live on in security as Norvis peKrin Dmorno.

Norvis waited impatiently for the return of the *Balthar*. The quicker he got off the land and back to sea, the better he'd like it. He spent most of the time walking the streets and throwing ineffectual stones at swooping sea-lizards. At least that gave him some satisfaction; the small-brained flying seathings were similar to the stupid peasants of Gelusar—nothing on their minds but food and the following of their ancient instincts.

At the end of the third day, he saw a familiar face. Down at the end of the Fishermen's Docks, busily cleaning scales from a newly unloaded cargo of fish, was Ganz peKresh Danoy, the middle-aged swabhand from the *Balthar*.

"How come you're here?" Norvis asked. "Skip ship or something?"

The elderly ex-farmer was even more washed out than he had looked aboard ship. "No," he said. "When the ship rolled, I became sick." He demonstrated with a vivid gesture. "I am too old to learn to stay aboard a ship."

"Sorry to hear that," Norvis said sympathetically.

"What happened then?"

"It was impossible for me to remain aboard ship," Ganz said, "So Captain Del agreed to release me from my contract, pay me some money, and find me a job here on the docks. I am very grateful to him."

"Captain Del is a fine man," Norvis said. "I'm waiting for the *Balthar* to come back myself, right now."

"Oh? Then your venture in Gelusar didn't work out?" the peasant asked innocently.

Norvis grinned. "I'm afraid not. I'm hoping to get my berth back on the *Balthar*."

"That is sad," Ganz peKresh said. "Tell me: how is it, in the peych regions? Are many of the farmers being—being driven out?"

"Unfortunately, yes," Norvis said. "And it'll get worse. The Elders have their own farms treated with this stuff, and they're turning out enough peych to fill the warehouses. The small men like yourself who can't afford the treatment are being pushed out."

Ganz peKresh's faded face became even more unhappy looking. "I can't understand how the Great Light will permit His Elders to do such a thing."

"I don't know, either, Ganz peKresh," Norvis said. He pulled together his cloak. At this time of year, the wind blew in from the sea, directly through the narrow, rock-bound channel. The combination of the sharp winds whipping in and the pungent odor of fish was becoming a little too much for Norvis, and he decided he'd best move on.

"They are so wise," Ganz peKresh said reflectively. "They hold our world in their hands. They should see what they're doing."

"I guess there's no answer," Norvis said. "Not when the Elders are becoming so wealthy."

As Norvis turned to leave, Ganz smiled wistfully and said: "It's too bad the growth treatment can only be given to the few; how wonderful it would be if all farmers could share equally in its bounty."

"Yes," Norvis said politely, barely listening to what the old man had said. "Well, I must be moving on."

"May the Great Light bless you," Ganz peKresh said.

"May He illumine your mind," responded Norvis.

He had gone more than a hundred paces before he realized that the old farmer had given him the answer.

V

Norvis spent the next two weeks in his dingy hotel room, scribbling over page after page of calculations and formulae of the new mathematics he had learned at the Bel-rogas School, trying frantically to dig out of his memory the things he had striven so hard to forget for four years.

Fool! Why hadn't he seen it before? Of course, it simply wasn't done; it was unethical, dishonest, and a downright dirty trick. He grinned gleefully as he worked. Sure it was a low blow, but the Scriptures said: "Those who transgress the Law shall fall before other transgressors." That was justification enough.

Finally, after he had all his notes down and was absolutely sure they were correct, he had one more problem to solve. He knew he could make the new hormone, but he had to make more of it, and faster. And, if possible, cheaper.

Now, let's see. What's the thing that makes the process so slow? He considered: it's got to be fermented in the vats, and then . . .

The Earthman, Smith, had taught him the trick of examining a problem closely to see where the solution lay. It was an Earthman kind of thinking. The first thing to do was to see what the problem *really* was. "Get back to the basic concept," Smith would say over and over again.

Norvis hadn't tried to use the method in years, because he hated everything he'd learned at the School. But now he saw that that kind of thinking was necessary if he were going to beat a man who thought that way. Smith and Company were going to be tripped by their own feet.

When Captain Del peFenn Vyless strode down the gangplank of the *Balthar,* he saw a familiar figure standing on the deck. His weathered face broke into a grin.

"Hoy! Norvis peKrin! By the Light, I *thought* you'd be back; once the sea gets into a man's blood, it's there to stay!" He shook the younger man's hand heartily. "What happened in Gelusar? I heard they stoned a man to death there for blasphemy, I hope you didn't get mixed up in it."

"No; I'm still alive. I saw what could happen to a man who tries to stir up trouble that way, so I decided on different tactics."

"Oh, so? Still trying to buck the Council?" The sea captain shook his head. "That's like trying to dim the Great Light Himself. Give it up, my boy."

Norvis shook his head. "I'm not giving up yet. I've got an idea, Captain. I've got a little scheme that will make the Elders uncomfortable and make us some money at the same time. It may be a little underhanded, but it's perfectly legal. Do you want to hear it?"

"Won't do any harm to listen," Del peFenn said.

"Come along to the Seaman's Guild Hall. I'll stand you to a drink."

"Right."

The public room of the Guild Hall was crowded with sailors who were relaxing after long voyages or bracing themselves for a new one. Norvis and the Captain managed to get themselves a table, and after the drinks had been brought, Norvis began to outline his plan.

"You know this new hormone that's being used to make peych grow better and mature faster? Well, I've got the formula for making it."

"But I thought some kid from the School held a monop—"

"Sure," Norvis interrupted. "But what does a hereditary monopoly guarantee? It guarantees that if someone else makes the stuff, the owner of the monopoly must get the *same* profit as if he had made it himself, and the quality must be as good or better than the quality of the good turned out by the original monopoly holder. Naturally, most people don't try infringing because they won't be able to get any profit. And if they do find a method of making it more cheaply, the original monopoly holder soon finds out about it, changes his own methods, and cuts out the newcomer by reducing his price and getting the same profit."

"Certainly," snorted Del peFenn. "But what good does that do us?"

"Well, I've got a method of producing the stuff that is cheaper than the Dran peNiblo process, and it requires an entirely different kind of factory. In order to do it our way, they'd have to scrap most of their present factory and rebuild entirely. That will take time and money, and by then we will have made our own little pile."

"I'll grant that, but reluctantly," the Captain said.

"Go ahead."

"All right; the way I see it, we'll make the hormone cheaper than the Gelusar plant is turning it out, and we'll sell it to the small farmers. We can give it to them at a lower cost, and still make enough to pay Dran peNiblo his proper profit, thereby keeping within the Law. That way, the schemes of the Earthmen will bounce right back on them, and we'll keep the Elders from becoming too powerful. We might even be able to drive the Gelusar manufacturers out of business, in which case, the monopoly will revert to us! All we need is a handful of men who will keep our process secret."

The Captain looked highly skeptical. "I've got men on my ship I'd trust anywhere," he said. "But how do you propose to do it? And what makes you think you have the right formula? And how can you produce more of it than the Gelusar plant can?" He gestured with a sinewy hand. "Why, it took several of the Council Elders to put up enough money to build that one little plant. How can we build more than that? I don't have that kind of money, Norvis. Nor do you."

Norvis stilled the Captain's rising flood of objections by raising his hand. "I'll prove that I know the right formula by making some for you. We'll try it on some peych and see.

"As for building a producing plant, I've got a new idea, as I said. A different way of doing things."

"How?" The Captain seemed a little more interested now. His hard, keen eyes were wide open.

"The trouble with the Gelusar plant is that it produces the stuff in big lots, which ties up all their equipment for weeks at a time. They use what's called a 'batch process' to turn it out. Now, if you can get the men on the ship to chip in with us, we can build the right kind of plant—one that will produce the stuff in a steady stream.''

The Captain blinked. ''The *men* chip in? But they haven't much money! It's unheard of!''

''They don't have much individually, but they have a lot collectively. We'll promise each man a share according to the amount he puts in, you see. That way, we'll get enough money, and if they have an interest in profits, they won't be likely to give our secret away.''

''That makes sense,'' the Captain agreed. ''But what about this new process? I don't see—''

Norvis pulled out a sheaf of papers covered with sketches and with explanatory notes in a large, scrawling hand. ''See here; we make the process continuous instead of whipping up batches. Instead of making one big glob at a time, we'll start the process at this end and feed in the various ingredients at different points along the line. Then we—''

He spent the better part of the afternoon explaining it, and when he was through, he looked up at the Captain. ''Well, what do you say?''

Del peFenn scowled. ''To be honest, there was an awful lot that I didn't understand. But it sounds as though you know what you're talking about.'' He paused while Norvis anxiously watched him chew over the idea in his mind. Finally, Del said: ''What you want is a sort of regular contract. You supply the brains, and the men and I supply the money. Fifty-fifty.''

Norvis nodded.

''I'm sorry,'' said the Captain, ''I just can't risk—''

Norvis stopped him. ''Now, wait a minute. You're the one who's taking the risk; I'll grant that. So I tell you what you do; you take control, too.''

''What's that?''

"You see to the buying of the equipment and everything. I'll just tell you what I want and how much I'll need. For my part of it, you can pay me a salary— whatever you think I'm worth. I trust you."

The Captain chewed that over, too. Hesitatingly, he said: "Well-l-l—I don't know. It sounds good, but— well, how much would it take?"

"Better than half a manweight," Norvis admitted.

Captain Del peFenn winced and shook his head. "More than forty thousand weights! I don't know. Let me think about it for a while."

It took Norvis better than a week to talk the sea officer into investing his money and recommending to his men that they put their own savings into it, but during that time he bought some small flasks and a few other things and ran off a batch of the hormone right under the Captain's eyes. The process worked just as Norvis had theoretically constructed it, back at Belrogas.

There were only a few drops, but it was enough. Norvis bought two potted peych seedlings and sprayed the stuff over the leaves of one, where it was absorbed by the stomata and went into the circulatory system of the plant.

"One thing we'll have to warn our customers about," Norvis said, "is using too much of the hormone. They'll tend to overdose at first, and if they do, they'll not only waste it, but probably ruin the plants."

"You've got this stuff figured out pretty well," Del peFenn said. "I knew you were sharp, but I didn't think you were as good as all that."

"Hold it," Norvis admonished. "Let's wait and see how sharp I am before you go passing out compliments like that. We'll know, one way or another, in a few days.''

When, within a space of five days, the treated plant was noticeably different from its twin, Captain Del peFenn decided it was time to sink his money into the new project.

Three months later, the first substantial yield from the new process came through the factory hidden in the foothills of the Ancestral Mountains near one of the smaller rivers in Pelvash Province. Norvis and Del were confronted with the stuff early one morning, when Drosh peDrang Hebylla, the tall, thin young man who was the foreman of the factory, came dashing up the end of the dock and hailed the nearby *Balthar*.

"Here it is!" he cried enthusiastically, after the dinghy had conveyed him from shore to ship. He leaped out and held up a small wooden box.

Norvis took it, lifted the lid, sniffed, and replaced the lid. "Ugh," he grunted, "it's not going to be its lovely odor that'll be the selling point, I'm afraid."

"You should come out and spend some time at the factory," said Drosh peDrang. "If you think this sample has a bad smell, you ought to hover around the end of the feed line for a while."

"That's all right," Del peFenn boomed. "There must be something in the Scripture someplace about being able to put up with nasty smells for the sake of turning an honest few weights."

Norvis thought for a moment. "No; I can't think of any."

"Nor can I," said Drosh peDrang.

"Nevertheless," the Captain maintained, "there must be something, something in that wonderful book to cover *everything!*"

"Well," said Norvis, "There's that part of the Fifteenth Section where Bel-rogas is lecturing against phony piety. He says: 'Appearances are nothing; it is the thoughts behind them that count. Often a sweet-smelling savor disguises a rotten evil beneath.' Well, if that's so, why not the other way round?"

The others laughed. "Why not, indeed?" said Del peFenn. "I think we have Scriptural backing for our project right there; we could probably find others."

"I wonder how the Elders are going to hide their red faces when we get our stuff out to the common people," Norvis said.

"They're not going to like it much," said Del. "But I think we'll be able to step on their toes so hard that it'll hurt for a long time." He turned to Drosh peDrang. "How long will it be before that 'sweet-smelling savor' is ready to ship?"

"The men should be packing the first load now," the foreman told him. "The barges will start down river to here as soon as they're loaded."

"Good. We'll take the *Balthar* to Lidacor as soon as we get her loaded; we might as well start distributing it at once. The people up there are so hungry they'll hail us as saviors."

"Fine," said Norvis. "Lidacor's a good place to begin. Besides, it'll be pleasant to get away from the eternal fish odor here in Vashcor. I like Lidacor."

"Oh, I forgot to tell you," Captain Del said. "You're not going with us, Norvis."

"How so?" Norvis asked, puzzled and a little disappointed.

"You're heading in the other direction, taking a cargo of the stuff to Molcor and Sundacor—and Tammulcor as well, I guess. You'll be aboard the *Krand*."

"The *Krand*? That's Captain Prannt peDel Kovnish's ship, isn't it?"

"It was," Del corrected. "It's now Captain Norvis peKrin Dmorno's. I entered your name on the Roll of Captains this morning. It's my new ship. I've decided to expand operations, now that there's the prospect of good business ahead. I'm now a two-ship man, and I couldn't think of a better captain for my new one than you, Norvis."

"I'm very grateful," said Norvis sincerely. He was tempted to add something of the Great Light, but decided against it; it wouldn't carry much weight in thanking Del, who didn't seem to set much store by the Scripture.

"You're sailing west with the second load, then," Del told him. "We ought to return rich men."

Norvis grinned. "Even with the share we'll have to give the Gelusar company, we'll make more profit than they will."

Del nodded. "And we ought to be able to get rid of the first two loads in no time."

They did. The hungry farmers of Sugon practically swarmed all over the *Balthar* as soon as word went round that a ship had arrived bearing the same wonderful mystery that had resulted in such marvelous production on the Elders' farms.

Del peFenn found people bidding frantically for the cargo, and one rich land-owner offered to buy the whole shipment for use on his farms. But Del kept in mind the carefully laid plan of Norvis peKrin, which was to distribute the hormone evenly according to acreage, and he resolutely held the price down and rationed out the quantity. He returned to Vaschor with an empty hold and a full purse.

As for Norvis, his first experience as captain of his own ship was an equally successful one. He guided the *Krand* flawlessly around the coast, heading in a westerly direction toward the southwestern port of Sundacor, and at each of the three stops along the way he disbursed a part of his cargo.

Del peFenn had been back in Vashcor for several days when the *Krand* returned. As soon as his ship was docked and anchored, Norvis made his way to the *Balthar*, but was told that the Captain was at the hormone factory.

A swift deest-ride took Norvis there. It was a tall and fairly imposing building, and he allowed himself the luxury of a sensation of pride at the sight of it.

He entered, and a busy-looking workman directed him up the stairs and around a corridor, where he opened a door and found Captain Del in conference with Foreman Drosh peDrang.

He sniffed as he entered. "It doesn't smell any better in here than it does in the rest of the plant."

The two men, startled, looked around. "Norvis!"

"Hoy, Del. How was business?"

Hurriedly, the two men spilled out to each other the story of the success of their respective voyages.

"It's going well, isn't it?" Norvis said. "Good, good. We'll teach the Elders they can't corner a valuable commodity like this and expect to keep it cornered." He turned to Drosh peDrang. "How are the local sales going?"

"We've established a center in Elvisen," he said. "The farmers have been coming from all over Pelvash to buy the stuff. The money's coming in faster than we can get it into the bank."

"Hmmm. We don't want to get *too* rich out of this

thing," Norvis said slyly. "Next thing we know, the Elders will be coming to us, looking for a loan."

"What's wrong with that?" Del asked.

"Looks bad in the public eye," explained Norvis. "The people are pretty much sold on the Elders, and we don't want to appear to be showing them up too badly. Remember what happened to that prophet fellow in Gelusar."

"The one they stoned?" said Del. "Well, they were right to stone him, I think. Wasn't he saying that the hormone should be abolished altogether?"

Norvis nodded uneasily. He was sure that Del was unaware that he was addressing that very prophet, but he wanted to make sure that the Captain never found out. Norvis peRahn Brajjyd was better off where he was.

"Well," the Captain said, "no wonder they stoned him. He was a false prophet, to say that the hormone should be abolished. That's an evil and stupid way to solve the problem! Give it to everyone! That's what he should have said."

"It probably didn't occur to him," Norvis said. "The poor devil! He didn't have enough brains to see the right way to handle the stuff— that's why they stoned him."

"I don't know why you're so sympathetic," Del peFenn boomed. "After all, doesn't it say in the Scripture that a false prophet shall be stoned? Doesn't it? I think I'm right, this time."

"You are," Norvis said. "Seventh Section. 'And men will come who will rise up and preach to the people, but unless they agree with the people, they will be called false prophets, and the people will stone them and kill them.' There was a dispute over the exact meaning of the passage a hundred cycles back, as to whether it was a prophecy or a command. The Council ruled that it was a command; they said that to call it a prophecy would eventually lead to heretical teachings.''

Del was impressed. "You're quite a scholar, aren't you?''

"I've done a little reading," Norvis admitted casually. To change the subject, he got up and walked to the window. "The point I was trying to make is that we mustn't antagonize the people by openly pitting ourselves against the Council. That's why we have to give full credit for our own operations to the Dran peNiblo Sesom plant in Holy Gelusar. We get the money, they get the credit.''

Del scowled. "Well, I did as you said, but I don't like it. Those farmers took our stuff and went away full of praise for the Elders.''

"Be satisfied with the money," Norvis said. "The Elders will get their comeuppance when the new crops ripen." He pointed out the window at the view of the rolling farmlands of the province of Pelvash. "Looks like they've got all their fields treated.''

The fields were bright with the blossoms of the peych plants. It was easy to see that the hormone was already in active use by the local farmers.

"Yes," said Drosh peDrang. "Sales have been tremendous—just tremendous.''

Norvis smiled. "It's going to be quite a surprise to the Elders when that harvest starts ripening all over Nidor, isn't it? They're not going to like it at all.''

"At least we've broken their stranglehold," Del said. "And we've given those Earthmen something to think about, too.''

"I'll say." Norvis looked out at the spreading gray-

green plains, the fertile hills with the tributary of the
Vash River wandering lazily among them. On every
hill and in every valley, the golden blossoms of the
peych shone, bright harbingers of the future.

It occurred to Norvis as he stood there that a couple of
men had engaged in blunt rebellion against the Earthmen and succeeded. For the first time, possibly, in the
history of Nidor, a man, an ordinary man, had taken the
course of action into his own hands. And the Great
Light still smiled upon him.

VI

"Wiped out!" shouted Captain Del peFenn Vyless. *"Ruined! Destroyed!"*

The *Krand*, her sails taut with the wind that pushed her across the scudding sea, vibrated with the sound of her owner's voice, and shook with the sound of his angry footsteps.

"The *Balthar*—burned! The factory—burned! Four of my best men—dead! Darkness take every one of the moronic sons-of-deests who did it!"

"That'd be about three-quarters of the farmers of Nidor," said Captain Norvis peKrin Dmorno. "What would we do for food without the farmers?"

The two men were sitting in the Captain's Cabin of the *Krand*—or, rather, Norvis was sitting; Del sat only for restless moments before he rose again to pace the gently moving deck.

Del peFenn whirled on Norvis. "What would we eat? Great Light, man! There's plenty to eat! The warehouses are full of peych-beans! The plants are rotting in the fields! Something to eat? Go grab yourself a handful! A basketful! Nobody will begrudge you a few worthless peych-beans!

"Or perhaps you'd like a steak. Go grab yourself a nice, fat, yearling deest! Nobody would mind—least of all the farmer who owns it! The only thing it's good for is to eat up the excess peych and breed more food-deests! And the Light knows we don't need any more food-deests!"

Norvis remained silent. In the year since the first great crop of hormone-charged peych had been harvested, the economy of Nidor had literally fallen apart. The first crop had more than filled the storage warehouses, it had filled the bellies of beast and man. And still there were tens of thousands of manweights of the crop lying unsold and unused in the farmers' bins, and more yet lying unharvested in the fields.

For more than two hundred cycles of years, the amount of the staple crop that the populace was capable of using had been exactly equal to the amount grown. In lean years, the slight excesses which had been put in the warehouses during the fat years were used. And no year was either excessively fat or excessively lean.

In years gone by, an excess of peych had meant an increase in the number of hugl, which meant a decrease in the following year's peych crop.

But where were the hugl now? Where were the millions of little animals that would gladly eat the vast excesses of peych that flooded Nidor?

They were dead—killed by Edris powder that was dumped regularly into the ponds and shallow lakes to prevent their breeding. Only a few could be found in out-of-the-way ponds.

Del peFenn had turned his back and was staring out a porthole. Norvis stared at that back without actually seeing it.

First Grandfather Kiv, he thought, *and now me. Is there a curse on our family, that we only help to destroy our culture when we try hardest to aid it?*

"One thing I'll say," said Del peFenn without turning, "is that we did at least part of what we set out to do. The people have at least shown those fool Elders that the Council isn't always right. If the Council had paid attention when they were petitioned, the farmers wouldn't have burned the Gelusar hormone factory."

And mercilessly hanged poor little Dran peNiblo Sesom, Norvis thought. For the first time in nearly six years, he no longer hated nor envied the man who had been given credit for Norvis peRahn Brajjyd's discovery. And that was only right; why should Norvis peKrin Dmorno carry on the hates and frustrations of a dead man?

Del said: "You know, maybe that false prophet they stoned to death was right, after all."

"How so?" Norvis asked, somewhat startled that Del should bring up the subject that had been on his own mind. It took him half a second to realize that the conversation had been heading inevitably in that direction, anyway.

"Well, maybe he saw something we didn't," said the sea captain, turning again from the porthole. "Maybe he saw that too much food is just as bad as too little; maybe he saw what overproduction of peych would do."

I wish he had, thought Norvis. Then, aloud, "If you ask me, Del, overproduction is worse. When men are hungry, they work together to produce more. When they have more than enough they squabble among themselves."

"Yes," said Del bitterly, "and they ruin and destroy our factory and our ship. Our holdings have been completely wiped out!''

Norvis stood up. "Darkness take it, Del!'' he said angrily. "Don't you see that you've nothing to complain about? Nothing! What have we lost? A factory that was useless to us, anyway. Did you think we could go on making money by manufacturing growth hormone? We haven't made a bit of the stuff for thirty days. What good was the factory?''

"What good are men's lives, eh? What good was the *Balthar?*'' Del's voice was harsh. "I suppose their loss was negligible, too?''

"By comparison, yes!''Norvis snapped. "We lost four good men, and I'm sorry; I'll see that the Service is said for them. But they weren't the only ones to die! There have been murders and mobbings all over Nidor! As many as a dozen coffins at one time have been in a Temple while the priest said a common Passing Service for them all! Four men? They are nothing by comparison!

"And the *Balthar!* It went to the torch, sure— because there was a load of spices aboard, and you wouldn't sell. What if you'd had a load of the hormone aboard? Do you think you'd have gotten away so easily? A lot more than four men would have lost their lives, believe me!''

"How could I sell?'' Del exploded. "They offered nothing but peych in exchange!''

"Then you should have given it for peych! You'd have kept your ship, and saved four lives as well!''

Del's eyes glittered dangerously. "Now you—''

He was interrupted by a knock on the cabin door.

"Who is it?'' Del roared.

There was a momentary silence, then a small, high-pitched voice said: "It's me, sir; Kris peKym.''

Norvis gave Del a silencing glance. Then, "Come in, Kris."

The door came open, and a small boy entered. He was carrying a tray which was laden with two plates of food and two large mugs of peych-beer. He looked up, wide-eyed, as though terrified by the glowering face of Captain Del.

"Don't just stand there, Kris," Norvis said in a kindly tone. "Captain Del isn't going to beat you—are you, Del?"

"No, of course not," the old sea-captain said gruffly.

"Go put the tray on the table, Kris," Norvis ordered. "Then go back to the galley. Captain Del and I are busy."

The boy walked over to the table and gingerly lowered the tray to its surface.

"How old are you, boy?" Del asked suddenly.

The lad jumped. "E-Eight, Ancient One."

"Aren't you a bit young to go to sea?"

Little Kris didn't answer; he turned and looked at Norvis.

"As long as he does his job well, he's old enough," Norvis said. "Now you get back to the galley; that's part of doing the job right—start the next job as soon as you've finished one. Run!"

The boy nodded and did as he was ordered. His little legs pistoned under him as he ran out the door, stopped, closed it, and ran on down the companionway.

"Why'd you take on so young a kid?" Del asked curiously. "Won't his parents raise Darkness?"

"Del, there's a perfect example of what I've been talking about," Norvis said. He sat down and pulled his share of the food toward him. "His parents were farmers. They're dead, both of them. Marauders from the city came out and took everything of value from their farm and killed them both. That left the kid with nothing but an empty farm and a barnful of peych.

"With nothing but a pair of shoes on his feet and a pair of shorts on his body, he headed for Tammulcor to make a living for himself—at *eight*. He didn't have a weight in his pocket, nor a vest to cover his chest."

"And you took him on?"

"I took him on. Where else could he go?" Norvis said nothing about feeling that he had a certain responsibility for the lad because it had been his fault, indirectly, that little Kris's parents had died; Norvis didn't want to bring up *that* subject!

Del nodded. "You're right, I suppose. The life's not bad for a hardy lad, and he looks as though he could take it." He rubbed a palm over the graying down on his forearm. "Just lit out for himself, eh? That takes nerve."

"Exactly. Look at what we have. The *Krand*, here, is still in perfect shape; we've got the new *Vyothin* ready to come off the ways; we've got plenty of money in the bank—good, hard cobalt; we've got merchandise stored away—bronzewood, spices, metals, laces, ornamental building stone, deest leather—all of them still worth money. We're not ruined. We've taken a devil of a beating, yes; but we're not ruined. We're not as well off as we thought we'd be, but we've got more than we had a year ago, in spite of our losses."

Del lifted his mug of brew and sipped thoughtfully. "That sounds good, Norvis, but it seems to me that the merchants will be as bad off as the farmers in another half-year."

Norvis nodded. "They will be—if you and I don't do something."

Del looked up from his mug. "Do something? What?"

"Look at it this way, Del; things are in a pretty mess right now; they're going to get worse. Not because they have to get worse, but because the Law and the Way aren't equipped to cope with something like this. Our Ancestors knew plenty about not having enough food, but they never put down a word in the Scriptures about having too much. Even the Great Lawyer, Bel-rogas Yorgen, didn't envision anything like this, which proves to me that the Earthmen aren't from the Great Light."

The older captain spread his hands. "If the Law can't cope with it, what can you and I do?"

"Make some changes, so that the Law *can* cope with it!"

Del scowled. "Now look here, Norvis! I don't have much use for that senile bunch of old Liturgy-chanters in Gelusar, but—change the Law? *The Law?* You can't do that; they'd have you hanging or stoned to death within a day after you started."

Norvis shook his head. "Listen to me; I didn't say anything about changing the Law. The changes I want to make are in applications of the Law.

"I remember you once said that *anything* could be proven by Scripture. Well, that's not absolutely true. You've got Scripture, the Ancestral Traditions, and the Law to worry about. But even so, changes in application can be made—they have been made before, except that they took so long that no one noticed them. The difference is that we need a lot of changes, all at once."

"How do you propose to do it?"

"You pointed that out yourself. The merchants will be the next to get cut down with the peych-knife. But if all the merchants band together and demand changes—changes that will help the farmer, now, when they need it, we'll have the peasants on our side, too.

"You're a well-known, respectable merchant-seaman. When we get to Vashcor, you call all the merchants together and give them our proposals; they'll listen to you."

"But what *are* our proposals?" Del asked, puzzled.

"I'll write them out, and we can talk them over on the way. I think we can make the Council listen to us; they're in pretty bad odor right now because they backed this hormone business. It's a good thing we kept our names out of it, or we'd be in the same kettle.

"Don't you see it, Del? If we can get the merchants *and* the farmers behind us, we can have the Elders jumping to *our* tootling, instead of the Earthmen's!"

"What are you going to be doing while I'm organizing the merchants?" There was a light in Del's eye, now—a light of excitement. He was beginning to see what could be done.

"Me?" Norvis grinned. "I'm going to be out buying up every bit of peych I can get my hands on."

"Peych? Are you crazy? What will you do with it?"

"Put it in warehouses, dump it in rented vacant lots—anyplace I can find."

Del looked dazed. "You've lost your mind. What are you going to do with all those beans?"

"Not just the beans, Del!" Norvis corrected. "Everything. Stalks, leaves, stems, chaff, hulls—everything."

"But they'll rot!"

"I hope so; they won't be much good if they don't."

"Norvis, dammit, don't sit there grinning like an overfed food-deest!! What in Darkness are you talking about?"

"Fertilizer, Del, fertilizer."

"Fertilizer?" Del slammed his palm down on the table. "What do you need fertilizer for?"

"Have you seen the new peych-bean crop?" Norvis asked softly. "It isn't even going to blossom. The soil is worthless. Do you know how farmers have fertilized their soil for thousands of years? They've raked up the muck from the bottom of the pond that every farm had. That muck came from hugl which died at the bottom after stuffing themselves with peych.

"To the muck, the farmer adds manure from his deest-barns, and other wastes are mixed in too. Then he plows the whole mess into the ground.

"But the muck has been poor lately because of the decrease in hugl; ever since Elder Brajjyd found a new way to use Edris, the muck has become more and more worthless.

"This hormone just did the final dirty work. The soil was overburdened depleted of its organic content when the fast-maturing, overabundant, hormone-treated peych was grown on it.

"Oh, we'll need fertilizer, all right. That's one of the things we're going to get passed by the Council of Elders—an order for the farmers to plow their old peych back into the ground."

Del finished his mug of beer and sat for several minutes staring at the empty container. Finally, he said: "I think we can do something, at least. Yes, I think we can. Now, what proposals did you say you wanted to make?"

The sign on the door of the big building in Vashcor said: *Merchants' Council Headquarters*. It was an imposing looking building; it had stood for hundreds of years, and had been newly redecorated with an imposing symbolic façade.

Outside of the Great Temple of the Holy Light at the Holy City of Gelusar, it was probably the most important building on Nidor.

In an inner office, Norvis peKrin Dmorno, Secretary of the Merchants' Party, sat behind a wide bronzewood desk and folded his hands together. "As a manufacturer, Gasus peSyg," he said, "I think you can see the point. You make cloth from peych-fiber; if people have too little money, they can't buy clothing, no matter how cheap it becomes, because they will have even less. You've got to keep your purchases of the raw material down, and keep the prices up. That means that you shouldn't buy any more from a given supplier than you bought five years ago, and you have to pay the same amount.

"That, in turn, will discourage overproduction, at the same time keeping prices on an even keel."

The heavy-set man with the steel-gray facial hair nodded. "As long as I have the backing of the other merchants, Secretary Norvis, I'll comply with the rules." Norvis nodded. "You back them, they back you. That's what the Council is for."

"Actually," Gasus peSyg continued, "I'm not being offered too much really good fiber these days. A lot of the stuff that's brought in is fiber that's been laying around in storage since the Year of the Double Crop, and fiber that's two years old isn't good for much. I've just been buying the fresh fiber, and that comes in in about the same quantities as I used to get."

Again Norvis nodded. "Things are evening up. You're doing exactly right; force them to sell the old stuff for fertilizer. The land is getting back into shape now, but there's still areas where work needs to be done."

The cloth manufacturer stood up. "Well, I'm glad

we got that little bit straightened out. Thank you, Secretary Norvis.''

Norvis smiled. ''Not at all, Gasus peSyg; that's what we're here for—to help the merchant and the farmer— or rather to help them help themselves and see that their rights are protected. Thank you for coming.''

The broad chested merchant headed for the door and almost collided with a tall young man who had hurriedly opened the door from the outside. They offered mutual apologies, and the young man waited until the merchant had closed the door after him before he said anything to Norvis.

''What is it, Dom?'' Norvis asked.

''There's an acolyte out here to see you, sir!''

''An acolyte?''

''Yes, sir; he says he represents the Elder Danoy!''

''Show him in.'' Norvis leaned back in his chair and smiled as the young man went out.

Well, well, he thought to himself, *what have we here?*

The Elder Danoy was the oldest priest in the Council now, and therefore automatically Elder Leader. The merchants' Council had been putting pressure on the Council of Elders for over a year now, and each time, they had acquiesced to the merchants' demands—but only stubbornly and unwillingly. Was there, perhaps, a change in sight?

The door opened, and a broad-shouldered, yellow-robed acolyte stepped inside. ''Secretary Norvis pe-Krin Dmorno?'' he asked, as he closed the door behind him. ''I am First Acolyte to Elder Grandfather Prannt peDran Danoy, Elder Leader of the Council of Elders of Nidor.''

Norvis rose. *He makes it sound impressive,* he thought. ''Yes, I'm Secretary Norvis,'' he said aloud.

"Please be seated, Acolyte." He indicated the chair which had recently been vacated by the merchant.

"Thank you." The yellow-clad man seated himself, and Norvis sat down again behind his desk. "I was told to see Leader Del peFenn Vyless, but I understand that he is at sea, and that you are empowered to speak for him."

"That's right, I am . . . ah" Norvis smiled. "I don't believe you gave your name."

"Gyls peDom Danoy," said the acolyte. "It is unimportant; I am here only as a voice for the Elder Grandfather. His age is such that he cannot travel the long distance from the Holy City to Vashcor, so I speak as Elder Leader in his stead."

"I see. I shall respect your words as such, Acolyte Gyls peDom."

"And I shall respect your words as being those of your Leader. May the Great Light illumine our minds, and those of our superiors."

"And may the Way of our Ancestors prevail," responded Norvis.

"To begin with," the acolyte began abruptly, "the Elder Leader wants it understood that he—ah—greatly deplores the tactics that are being used by your organization. You have cast doubt upon the wisdom of the Elders; you have attempted to subvert the people's confidence on our Holy Government; you are upsetting the administration of the Law by advocating countless written petitions to the Council; you have preached falsely against the Council and the Earthmen; you—"

Norvis held up a hand. "One moment, Acolyte! How have we preached falsely against the Council?"

Gyls peDom widened his eyes, as though astonished that Norvis should ask such a question. "You have said publicly that the Council was reluctant to co-operate in the rehabilitation of Nidor after the terrible decimation caused by the unwise use of the growth hormone two and a half years ago. You have blamed the use and invention of the hormone on the Earthmen and claimed that the Council was duped into allowing its use. Do you deny that your organization has said these things?''

"No," Norvis admitted. "And the question of whether they are true or not, we will leave for later."

The acolyte looked at him through narrowed eyes for a moment, as though he were going to argue then and there. Apparently, he thought better of it; his eyes relaxed, and he went on in the same tone of voice as he had used before.

"To sum up; your entire program has been offensive to the Divine Priesthood, detrimental to the spiritual health of the people, and displays such disrespect and irreverence toward the Great Light Himself as to border on sacrilege and blasphemy.

"This attitude is intolerable to His Effulgence's Holy Government. You are therefore—" He reached inside his yellow robes and withdrew a sealed, embossed, official-looking paper. "—commanded, by order of the Council of Elders, to cease, desist and discontinue any and all such unholy practices, either by the spoken or written word, or by actions tending to have the same effect. This applies both to direct insults and to indirect suggestions, insinuations, and innuendoes.

"Is this fully understood?"

Silently, Norvis opened the official document and read it. It was, if possible, couched in even harsher terms than those the acolyte had used, but it said essentially the same thing.

"All right," Norvis said quietly, "the Council has gone on record as making an official protest. What else?"

Gyls peDom spread his hands. "That's all. Henceforth, you will simply bring your suggestions to the Council, where they will be properly handled; they must be debated and justified with the Law and the Way. Contrary to the statements made in your public vilification of the Holy Council, the Elders are most anxious to see that Nidor be returned to its former state of peace and tranquility. They are aware that extraordinary measures must be taken. Representing, as you do, the merchants and many of the farmers, your advice is considered valuable, though certainly not indispensable. You must not, however, make the mistake of thinking that you *are* Government; such presumptuousness is so insulting to the Great Light Himself that it can only end in disaster—for you, and for all Nidor."

Outwardly calm, Norvis leaned back in his chair. "I can well understand that, Acolyte Gyls peDom. Naturally, such a decision on policy change will have to be carefully considered, but, I think you can rest assured that the wishes of the Holy Council will be complied with. We have no wish to undermine the influence of the Ancient Elders; as a matter of fact, we had already considered that perhaps our stand might be a little too strong, and now that we see that it is, shall we say, much stronger than necessary, I'm quite sure our policies will be adjusted accordingly."

"Excellent." The acolyte arose. "There is, then, nothing more to be said. You will be expected to communicate with the Elder Leader, in writing, within the next twenty days. The peace of your Ancestors be with you always."

"And may the Great Light illumine your mind as he does the world, Acolyte," Norvis replied.

Without another word, the yellow-robed figure

turned and walked out the door. His message had been delivered.

For a full minute, Norvis sat, unmoving, his face expressionless, listening to the footsteps of the acolyte recede. Not until he heard the faint clatter of deest-hooves on the pavement outside did he throw back his head and shout.

"Hoy*hoy*!" he chortled gleefully. "Total capitulation! Absolute surrender! Hoy*hoy*hoy!"

The Council had saved face, but the essence of the message was simply: "If you'll shut up and stop all this rabble-rousing propaganda, we'll do what you say."

There was a rap at the door, and the young clerk put his head in. "Is something the matter, Secretary Norvis?"

"Matter?" Norvis stood up, vaulted over his desk, and did a little jig. "Something the matter? No! What could be the matter? The Great Light sheds His Brilliance over everything and comforts everyone! Nidor glows beneath His Effulgence! And you ask if anything is wrong! A shadow upon you, boy! A shadow upon you!"

The clerk, taken aback by this un-Norvis-like behavior, stepped back in wide-eyed astonishment.

Norvis stopped his antics, but kept his grin. "Dom, keep it in mind that a man can fail a thousand times, but if he keeps plugging, success may come from the most unexpected quarters!"

"Yes, sir."

"Now, attend," Norvis continued, "The *Krand* is due in this evening, just after lastlight. The rain will have started, but I want a man stationed down there, waiting for it, anyway. As soon as the ship pulls in, Captain Del peFenn is to be told to come here as quickly as possible; have a deest waiting for him, too.''

"Yes, sir.''

"And I don't want to see anybody else unless it's of absolutely vital importance. Understood?''

"Yes. Ancient One.''

"Fine. Go to it, then.''

The clerk backed out the door, still bewildered.

Norvis walked over to the window and looked out upon the busy streets of the harbor city. He had won. The Council was with him now; it was only a matter of time before the Earthmen were completely discredited, And then—

"And then, Smith," he said softly, "we'll see about you, personally.''

Outside the window, the Great Light, hovering near the horizon, began to dim.

AFTERWORD

By Robert Silverberg   June, 1980

In the summer of 1955 Randall Garrett, a 28-year-old writer with about a dozen published science-fiction stories, moved to New York City, and, through a complicated series of events, settled in the residential hotel where I lived. I was eight years younger, a junior at Columbia University, and was just beginning my own career as a writer. I had been writing seriously for a couple years, and had sold one novel and five short stories—a decent enough showing for a teenager, perhaps, although my total income thus far had been under $400—including the novel. Nevertheless, I was undeniably a professional writer, and so (although he was vastly more proficient) was Garrett. It wasn't long before we were talking about collaborating.

There was logic to such a collaboration, for we complemented each other admirably. Garrett had a keen sense of plot structure and a solid grounding in the physical sciences—which were two of my weaknesses as a writer. On the other hand, his style was rough and choppy, his ability to create complex characters was limited, and—most critical—he was going through a bad phase in his life in which his writing disciplines had broken down and he found it almost impossible to finish the stories he began. And there was I, ambitious, productive, already phenomenally prolific and disciplined, with a liberal-arts literary background, a good sense of character, and a smoothly flowing style. If we worked together, we saw, we would balance one another's flaws and produce work superior to what either of us was doing individually. The alternative was to go on as we had been—Garrett writing almost nothing, and I writing a great deal but selling only a fraction of it.

So we went into business together. Garrett took me downtown to visit the New York science fiction editor—Howard Browne of *Amazing*, Bob Lowndes of *Future*, Leo Margulies of *Fantastic Universe*, and John W. Campbell of *Astounding*. He introduced me as a bright young star and announced that we planned to stand the science-fiction world upside-down with a series of spectacular stories. And, very quickly, all of those editors were buying stories from us—perhaps not so spectacular, but publishable enough so that whatever we wrote found a market at once.

The editor who was the center of our attention was Campbell. Not only did he pay the highest rates in the field—3¢ a word, triple what most of the others offered—but he was the pivotal figure of modern science fiction, an editor of almost legendary reputation who had discovered and developed such writers as Robert A. Heinlein, Theodore Sturgeon, Isaac Asimov, A.E. van Vogt, L. Sprague de Camp, and L. Ron Hubbard. Garrett, who had written several excel-

lent stories for Campbell's magazine, revered him. And
to me he was an awesome, titantic entity, the editor of
editors; though I had been published in a number of
minor magazines, I felt I would not truly be a profes-
sional science-fiction writer until I had appeared in
Campbell's *Astounding*.

In one of our visits to Campbell's office he mentioned that he was having difficulties just then finding
novels to run as serials. The hint was clear; we were
young men of talent, ambition, and *hybris;* we went
home that hot summer afternoon determined to concoct
a novel for Campbell.

"Concoct" is the right word. Neither of us happened
to have, at the moment, an idea suitable for a major
story. So we began the process from the back end,
drawing on our knowledge of the sort of novel John
Campbell liked to publish, then attempting to invent a
story that would be similar to the usual *Astounding*
serial but different enough to merit publication. This is
not the recipe for great science fiction. In devising our
prototypical Campbell novel we had to filter out all
those serials with sparks of real individuality, stories
like Van Vogt's *World of Null-A* or Williamson's . . .
and Searching Mind or Kuttner's *Fury*. We wanted to
play it safe, to make the big sale. And what we came up
with was this:

*Earthmen are superior to alien life-forms. Earthmen
therefore may meddle with alien cultures at will, provided they are serving some higher goal. An acceptable
higher goal is to meddle with an alien culture for its
own good, especially if the meddling will also serve to
enhance the quality of Earth culture.*

Campbell seemed to have an insatiable appetite for
that theme. It was, one might say, the basic CIA story:
agents of Earth (meaning the United States of America)

tamper with the politics of other planets (countries) for the alleged good of everybody. Of course, we knew very little if anything about the CIA in those distant days; but the blueprint for every slick trick that agency carried out in the postwar era can be found in the crumbling pulp pages of *Astounding Science Fiction*, I'm certain.

All one sweltering weekend we constructed an outline for a three-part serial to our theme. The plot was intricate, the action fast and furious. Our protagonist was a Scot named Murdoch or McTavish or something like that—another example of our cunning sense of market savvy, for Campbell, of Scots ancestry himself, was known to believe that the highest forms of terrestrial intelligence had evolved somewhere north of Edinburgh. Down to his office we hurried, and with passionate intensity we told him our tale. He listened in dour silence, pausing occasionally to stuff a new cigarette in his cigarette-holder or to squirt his awesome nose with nasal spray. And when we were done he leaned back, studied our tense and earnest faces carefully, and said. ''Not bad. But you've got it all wrong.''

He proceeded to turn our story inside out—getting rid of McTavish entirely and making the aliens the protagonists, *something we had rejected as too unCampbellian an approach*. He invented the technique for cultural tampering on the spot—a school of theology. He took the solar system we had invented and rearranged it to serve the theme more effectively. We gaped as in five minutes he reconstructed, and vastly improved, all that we had done.

''Now go home and write it,'' he said. ''Oh— don't do it as a serial. I want a series of novelets.''

We staggered out, hurried to the subway, and by the time we were home had the outline of our story,

"The Chosen People," what is now the section titled "Kiv" in *The Shrouded Planet*. I worked out the plot of the story, Garrett most of the background, and he set to work on the first draft. Which of us wrote what is now, after twenty-five years, difficult for me to say; but I have no doubt at all that the opening paragraphs, with their sly spoof of pulp magazine narrative-hook technique, was his work, and that the final page of the story, with its hint at moral ambiguities, was mine. Beyond that I'm unable to assign responsibility for individual aspects of the story.

We finished it in a few days—11,000 words—and took it to Campbell one morning in August, 1955, stopping off en route at the Cathedral of St. John the Divine so that Garrett, a devout Anglican, could improve our luck with a bit of Holy Communion. Then we delivered the story, and, twenty-four fidgety hours later, got our verdict: Campbell was sending out a check for $330 and would we please get going on the sequel? Oh, and also, didn't we think "By Randall Garrett and Robert Silverberg" was an awfully cumbersome line for the table of contents? What about a pseudonym? "Robert Randall, perhaps," Campbell suggested.

I was mildly miffed at having my name disappear from the pages of *Astounding* so soon after it had arrived there—but, no matter, I was bound to sell something non-collaborative to Campbell sooner or later. The important thing was that he had taken the story. I was a Campbell writer at last! (And I lay awake all that night, mulling the awesomeness of it all.)

Excited or not, we had other stories to do for other editors, and two months went by before we delivered the second "Robert Randall" story to Campbell— "The Promised Land," we called it, now the "Sindi" section of *The Shrouded Planet*. To my horror,

Campbell insisted on reading it while we waited at his desk—all 15,000 words of it—but though he scowled and clenched his teeth from time to time, we knew we were safe when he made a small pencilled editorial change midway through the story, and he accepted it on the spot without requiring, as he had for the first story, any minor revisions.

Three months later we brought him "False Prophet"—the "Norvis" section of *The Shrouded Planet*. Campbell bought that too; but when we told him that we thought one more novelet of about 15,000 words would conclude the series, that diabolical editor sprang on us a surprise that I think he had been saving all along. He had seen what we could do at shorter lengths, and the three stories on hand would build reader interest nicely when he began publishing them a few months hence. Now, he said, we should end the series with a novel—a three-part serial, as we had originally intended!

I was now in my senior year at Columbia, and, though I was still managing to write short stories both on my own and with Garrett at a rate of three or four a month, a novel meant sustained effort of the sort I could not then find time to do. So we had to wait until the summer, after my graduation; and in August of 1956, in nine days of the most concentrated and exhausting work imaginable, we produced the 67,000-word novel *The Dawning Light*, writing in relays round the clock, sleeping when we could, one of us pounding out the first draft and the other revising it to final copy. We lurched down to Campbell with the manuscript, he read it with his usual promptness, and the check—my share was an enormous $904.50—arrived a few days later, just in time to pay for my honeymoon and the first month's rent on the apartment my bride and I had found on Manhattan's Upper West Side. I was 21 years old then, and, I think, the youngest writer ever to have a novel published in Campbell's magazine.

By then the first stories in the series had been published. They were popular with the magazine's readers, and shortly we had an offer from a book publisher—Gnome Press, a semi-professional outfit that by dint of its early arrival in the field had managed to acquire rights to the best works of Asimov, Heinlein, Arthur C. Clarke, Simak, Leiber, and other major writers. Gnome offered only a pittance, but that hardly mattered, considering the company we'd be keeping and the royalties we imagined would arrive over the years. We assembled the three novelets, along with some introductory and connective matter, into *The Shrouded Planet*, which was published in 1957; *The Dawning Light*, almost unchanged from its magazine version, followed in 1959. For a time we thought we would continue the series into a third volume, and we actually wrote one lengthy section, "All The King's Horses," in 1957, but for various reasons we never went beyond that point.

The Gnome Press books went out of print after a few years and are now rarities, and neither of the Robert Randall novels has been published again until this time. I confess that I was not very eager to see them come back into print, for I remember how cynically we went about the business of cooking up a story that would appeal to John Campbell, and how quickly the books were written, and how young and unseasoned we both were as writers. But as I look at them now I can see not only their obvious faults but also their virtues, virtues which made the stories popular in their own time and which justify editor Hank Stine's faith in reprinting them now. The books are not in the same class with

Garrett's fine later works—his Lord Darcy stories, for example—or, say, my own *Dying Inside* or *Nightwings*. But why should they be? Those are the products of skilled writers long at their trade; *The Shrouded Planet* and *The Dawning Light* are the less assured, less accomplished work of young men. That much allowance must be made for them. But, taken on their own terms, the books are fun. I think cagey old John W. Campbell knew what he was doing, when he turned our wily outline topsy-turvy and told us to go home and write a series of novelets from the viewpoint of the aliens.

—Robert Silverberg